Copyright © 2019 by Claire Duffy

All rights reserved.

No part of this book may be reproduced in any form or by any electronic or mechanical means, including information storage and retrieval systems, without written permission from the author, except for the use of brief quotations in a book review.

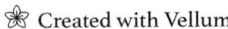 Created with Vellum

PRAISE FOR CLAIRE DUFFY

Well, well, well this book makes for a rollercoaster of a ride. This book throws you around like washing in a tumble dryer. Throwing twist and turns at you until right at the very end. When the author is ready to lay out what has exactly been happening in this book and then boom everything makes sense. Wonderful.

- **Karen W**

A brilliantly twisted psychological thriller that kept me guessing right to the end. The plot was dark and complicated, yet easy to read. There were twists aplenty and secrets in abundance. The characters were well thought out and original, their background was revealed slowly, adding to the suspense. The descriptive writing transported me with ease to another country and culture. A really good read.

- **Sarah K**

I loved this book. The story was compelling and fairly easy to follow. The story although complex is enthralling and I didn't work out 'the whodunnit' until near the end. Definitely a good read. I will look out for more by this author.

- **Lenore S**

Ellie, Ellie, Ellie. What a ride. Behind Blue Eyes by Claire Duffy seductively draws you in and then tosses you around like a sock in a dryer. I loved how descriptive the setting was. It was easy to get completely lost in the twisted tale. I can't wait for the next in the series.

-**Rachelle S**

BROKEN MIRRORS

CLAIRE DUFFY

CS DUFFY

1

Long after midnight, when the corporate events are over and the bars have emptied, the hotel sinks into silence with a contented sigh and Irina likes to imagine the guests fast asleep above her. Deep into the night she tidies the reception desk, lining up the pens and notepaper just so, ensuring the various computer cords aren't tangled, carefully polishing a single smudge on the gleaming walnut desk.

The stressed woman in the conservative business suit whose hand trembled as she signed her check in forms, Irina hopes she had a long, hot bath before slipping between the sheets and drifting into a sound sleep. The quiet guy in the leather jacket — some sort of musician, Irina gathered, from her younger colleagues — with the exhausted eyes and lost smile. She imagines him enjoying the late night burger he called down for in front of a cheesy movie he's seen twenty times already. The couple, older even than Irina, who held hands as they checked in, confided it was their fiftieth wedding anniversary. Irina sent them a complimentary bottle of champagne and wonders if they are still whispering in the dark, reminiscing about their wedding, the births of their children, long summers and Christmas dinners.

It is six o'clock in the morning, though in deepest winter, dawn is still a long way off. Irina delivers her handover report to the young man with the suspiciously shiny teeth who never quite looks her in the eye, then wraps herself warmly in her ancient winter coat. She carefully tucks her scarf into her collar so that not so much as a wisp of bitter air can invade, tugs her sleeves over her gloves and pulls her thick woollen hat as low as it will go over her ears. It's her favourite hat. She crocheted when she was on bed rest with her third daughter and bored out of her mind for four months. Last winter, she thought she had lost it for several weeks and was more than a little embarrassed by just how heartbroken she was.

Despite all these preparations, she lets out an involuntary gasp when she steps through the revolving door and a sharp gust of icy air hits her windpipe. Minus fifteen at least, she judges, taking a couple of slow, deep breaths to adjust to the cold. The tightness in her chest relaxes, and she decides, again, that she doesn't need to see a doctor just yet. Everyone is suffering this winter. It is only the second week of January, and already she can't remember when she felt a temperature above zero. It is good for her old lungs to have a little challenge, she tells herself grimly as she takes a step and her feet sink into deep, soft snow.

It has snowed heavily in the night, another half a metre or so. By the time she reaches the corner at the far end of the square she is sweating heavily with the exertion of wading through knee high snow. She stops for a moment, reminding herself that the T-bana stop is only another block or so away, and that in just over half an hour she will be at home in her cosy little apartment in Midsommerkransen. She will make a cup of hot tea and some buttery toast and take it to bed with her as a treat, she decides. She doesn't have to pick up her grandchildren until 3pm, she has plenty of time to sleep.

Cheered by the thought, she makes her way across Sankt Paulsgatan. Beneath the fresh snow is a layer of ice, several centimetres thick. She misjudges a step and skids and almost falls to her knees, cursing herself for not having the hiking poles she normally uses at this time of year. Enticing smells waft from the little bakery on the corner. Irina can just glimpse the rosy glow of the ovens behind the counter as she passes, baking the day's breads and buns.

Later, she will explain to the police that she has no idea what causes her to her turn around. She can't recall hearing a noise that caught her attention. She isn't thinking of anything in particular, except how much she was looking forward to getting home to tea and toast and bed, when she glances back at the square and her breath catches in her throat.

The figure is standing in the patch of grass next to the children's playpark. From across the road Irina can't tell whether it is a man or a woman, she can't even be certain it's a person. She creeps closer, barely noticing when snow drifts over the top of her snow boots and seeps into her trousers, though her arthritic knee will punish her later.

'Hello?' she calls when she reaches the path that separates the children's park from the patch of grass. 'Are you alright?' Her daughter would scold her for intruding, she thinks. *Leave people alone unless they ask for help, mamma,* Linda would tell her crossly, but Irina can't help it. Sometimes people are afraid to ask for help.

The figure doesn't respond, and Irina glances around

with a little prickle of nerves. *It's well after six now,* she thinks with a flash of irrational annoyance. People should be up, getting breakfast, on their way to work. She shouldn't be alone in the dark with this strange figure. What on earth is everyone doing still lying in bed?

The figure leans back slightly, their arms aloft in the air as though they are waving for help on a desert island or conducting an invisible orchestra. Irina's heart starts to beat faster as she sees that the figure is covered in snow, even its face. They must have been standing still during the entire blizzard.

That's ridiculous. She laughs, shaking her head, glad that no one was around to see an old lady get such a fright. She can't believe she thought it was a person standing there in the dark. It must be a statue, some kind of an art project or prank.

Probably something to do with the kids from the nearby high school, Irina thinks with a chuckle, annoyed at herself for making her journey that tiny bit longer and forcing herself to cross the treacherous road three times. At least the bakery opens at half past six. Seven more minutes and she will be able to get a coffee and a cinnamon bun fresh from the oven to warm the rest of her journey. That's what she'll do, in fact. She should thank the kids that played the prank, she thinks with a wry smile as she turns to cross the road a final time.

This time, she knows what catches her attention. Some snow, disturbed by a little flurry of birds flapping by just above the figure's head, crumbles to the ground, exposing its face. Irina's chest tightens again and she sees little black dots dancing at the edge of her vision.

The woman is beautiful. Delicate cheekbones, flawless skin glistening a pale blue in the moonlight. She stares with black eyes, watching coldly as Irina staggers towards her. 'There, there, it's okay —' Irina gasps, her chest tightening like a vice grip. 'I will call for help — you poor thing, what happened to you?' The woman must be trapped, somehow. Why won't she move? She is standing, her eyes are open, she must be conscious.

Fumbling in her panic, Irina struggles to get her coat off, dusts snow from the young woman's shoulders, wraps the coat around her. She moans out loud when her fingers brush her bare neck. The skin is so icy it almost seems frozen solid as Irina strokes her cheek, brushes her hair back from her face as she did to Linda when she was a little girl. 'You're alright now, I've got you,' she murmurs frantically as her heart pounds and the world spins. 'There is nothing to be afraid of. I'm here.'

The baker glances out his window and comes running. He finds little Irina, shivering uncontrollably without her coat. Her arms are wrapped around the dead girl and she is stroking her hair, promising her over and over that everything is going to be okay.

2

Icy air sawed at the back of my throat and I regretted everything. What on earth had possessed me to take up running, for heaven's sake? I had always held a healthy disdain for that province of creepy keen people who also stocked their kitchens with food they wouldn't be eating in the next few hours and were known to refuse a final glass of wine because they had had something called 'enough.' Clearly, this disdain had been entirely correct.

'Come on babe, look alive!' called my friend Maddie, from about a mile further down the road.

Last summer, Maddie had adopted me at a newcomers in Sweden club she ran. She and her girlfriend Lena had been there for me when I found a dead body on a remote archipelago island in the Baltic Sea that turned out to be my boyfriend's former girlfriend. I'd eventually unmasked one of his best friends Mia as the killer, but after I confronted her she disappeared. Five months later, she was still on the run.

Maddie was now studying to qualify as a personal trainer and dragged me out to exercise on an alarmingly regular basis. I was reasonably confident that she would kill me one of these days, but with one thing and another, I felt I owed her.

I had always vaguely liked the idea of being the sort of person who went for runs. Not enough to ever go for one, you understand, but I had occasionally pictured myself striding along through chilly afternoons, blood pumping, endorphins raging, just me, the elements and my thoughts. Turned out that the main thought I had was *fucking hell I hate running and I want to go home..*

'Are you not qualified enough to take on clients who actually want to do this yet?' I huffed when I finally caught up to her. 'Are you quite certain you still need to practice on me?'

'Positive,' she shrugged with a grin. 'I've got another set of exams yet, then there's a wait to find out if I've made the cut.'

'And you definitely don't want to become, like, a fire fighter or a candlestick maker?'

Maddie had been a lawyer in Australia. She insisted she had once been a corporate madam who'd strutted about Sydney in little suits with 'an actual bluetooth headset surgically attacked to my ear like a wanker,' but looking at her now, I couldn't picture it. Maddie was like a little ginger pixie with short red hair that poked in a billion different directions and whose dress sense was part vegan world traveller, part comedy tramp from black and white movies. She always looked a little bit mad and interesting, and I felt ever so slightly dull next to her, with my standard hair that just sort of hung more or less to my shoulders not doing anything interesting, and jeans and a jumper.

'I looked into doing some kind of legal consulting with firms who do business in Oz back when I first got here,' she'd told me once. It must have been early autumn, Johan was still in hospital after the fire during which Mia escaped. Maddie and I were sitting by the window of a coffee shop on Götgatan watching rain bouncing off the cobblestones outside. It was startling now to think that had just been a few weeks earlier. This winter had been so harsh that sometimes it felt as though the world had been frozen as long as I could remember.

'Obviously I can't fully practice here given that my Swedish seems stuck on telling people my name and that the sun is shining today,' Maddie continued, 'but I might have been able to keep my hand in somehow, work remotely or something if I'd really wanted to.'

She'd shrugged, toyed with a forkful of her carrot cake. 'But Lena suggested I just chill and settle in for the first few months, and by the time I started thinking about work I realised that Stockholm-Maddie doesn't wear little suits or care about a comma in clause 17.4.b until three in the morning, and I really prefer Stockholm-Maddie. I had long hair back in Sydney,' she grinned, running a hand through her short, spiky red hair. 'The money I've wasted on bloody blow outs over the years, it makes me want to weep. I Skyped my mum right after I got it cut and she burst into tears, said I looked like the real me. She's right. It's mad that I found the real me half a world away, but it is what it is.'

I'd looked away then, focussed on the glorious caramel-marshmallow-brownie concoction that was already making my teeth itch, trying to ignore the little wave of sadness that had washed over me.

I'd been a journalist since I left school, working my way up through making coffees and photocopying for what felt like eons, gradually scoring the odd freelance gig, before finally nabbing a staff job on a tiny local rag in North

London. It was so far from my stomping ground of Wandsworth that as the Northern Line trundled endlessly beneath the city I half expected to cross at least one passport check and be ordered for inoculations. A couple of years later, I made it on to the crime section of the Evening Standard and swore blind I would never step foot on the Northern Line as long as I lived.

I'd done alright. I'd paid my dues, got myself a handful of decent scoops that ensured commissioning editors accepted my calls when I went freelance a couple of years ago. I loved it. The thrill of chasing a story, the jubilation when a hunch comes together, the satisfaction of seeing some smarmy bastard nailed in black and white because I'd refused to give up. It was the only thing I'd been good at in my entire life, and I bloody loved every second of it. Then I met my dreamy Swede and hopped on a one way flight to Stockholm without a backwards glance.

It's not quite as pathetically anti-feminist as it sounds, though maybe don't ask me to explain precisely how just at the minute. In fairness, I had fondly imagined that long-distance freelancing would be a bit more doable than it had turned out to be. Problem was, for crime you need to be on the ground, doorstopping witnesses, thumbing through dusty archives that no one would ever get around to digitising, gathering outside the Old Bailey to see the accused with your own eyes.

I wasn't around to do that in London any more, and the language barrier meant I couldn't do it in Sweden. I'd padded my dwindling savings over the past few months with the odd bit of glorified blogging about life in Sweden and one series of corporate articles about anti-flammable chemicals which had paid a few bills and made my brain melt in despair and drip out of my ears. If I was going to stay in Sweden, I was going to have to figure out what I was going to be when I grew up, and pretty sharpish.

Obviously I was going to stay in Sweden, I mean. I just needed a job.

It was fine. I'd only been in Stockholm a few months, really. I was still finding my feet.

'What's going on there?' Maddie said now as she jogged alongside me. She was basically going in slow motion while I was pretty sure I was running for my life. My legs trembled and my lungs burned. The sweat on my forehead appeared to be frosting over, which was the most confusingly uncomfortable sensation ever.

I followed her gaze and something cold and hard slithered through my guts. At the end of the road in front of us, yellow crime scene tape fluttered in the light breeze. Powerful lamps glowed a harsh silver, making the darkness around seem even deeper. Scene of Crime Officers in their other-worldly white suits tramped to and fro between a tent that covered one corner of Mariatorget, and the various police cars and vans that were blocking Sankt Paulsgatan.

'Let's go that way,' I said, turning around. 'We can cut up by the old railway bit.'

'You don't want to see what's going on?'

'No,' I replied firmly, breaking into a run.

THE SMELL HIT me as I yanked open the brass concertina door of the elevator at the landing outside Johan's flat. Something spicy. That Moroccan stew he made in the fancy pot that looked like a tent and had a name I could never remember. My stomach was rumbling as I rummaged through my bag for my keys.

Leave it to Johan, I thought, feeling a little rush of affection tumble over me as I kicked off my shoes. The world may crumble around him, and he'll still be frowning at the stove, precisely measuring all manner of fiery coloured spices over melt-in-your-mouth-meat. I padded into the kitchen, my toes feeling numb and swollen as they fizzed and burned with the surprise of being warm.

Sure enough, Johan was leaning over the terracotta pot as though the burbling liquid contained the answer to the meaning of life. I reached up on tip toes to kiss him on the cheek. He ruffled my hair absentmindedly, then held out a spoon as I reached for the bottle of red on the counter.

'Is there enough turmeric in this?' he asked, as I obediently swallowed.

'I don't have a clue which one turmeric is,' I grinned, 'but it tastes lovely if that helps.'

He shrugged. 'I suppose it does.'

He turned the heat down, and accepted the wine I'd poured for him.

'How are you?' I asked, sitting at the kitchen table with my feet curled under me and watching him as he stirred the pot. There was that tightness to his jaw, his shoulders just a little too military straight, making him seem even taller than he actually was, which was pretty tall to begin with. His dirty blond hair was in its usual messy bun, a random curl yanked out where he must have wiped sweat from his forehead as he cooked.

'You haven't heard?'

Something in my stomach twisted. I took a sip of my wine. 'My phone died earlier,' I said. 'Is it Krister?' I asked. 'Is he okay?'

Krister had been Johan's best friend since the day they started school together at age seven. Krister and Mia had been together since they were in their mid twenties, until I discovered that she had murdered nine people, including Johan's two girlfriends before me, Liv and Sanna.

Krister had seemed relieved to begin with, free from the control Mia had held over him all these years, but as the months went by he had retreated into himself. I kept reassuring Johan that it was just a stage in his healing process, but the truth was, the last time I'd seen Krister he'd looked like a ghost and I'd been worried.

'I don't know. He is not answering his phone,' Johan said quietly. He dished out rice onto two shallow bowls and brought the stew to the table. 'He never answers his phone any more.'

'I'm sure he just needs space,' I muttered lamely.

Johan nodded. 'A murder victim has been found,' he said. He started to eat, feigning casualness, but I could see his knuckles whiten as he clutched his fork.

Shit. Tiny daggers of horror zipped over me. The crime scene at Mariatorget. I should have realised. I'd managed to identify several of Mia's victims, but I suspected there was many more. She was good at what she did.

'She was posed standing up in the snow like some kind of statue. They think she was dead for one or two days before being found.'

'Two days? So not —'

'Of course not Mia,' Johan snapped. 'This poor woman was murdered then posed like an ice sculpture by some kind of sick fuck. Of course not Mia,' he repeated quietly. He sighed, leaned back in his chair, ran a hand through his hair. 'I'm sorry. I did not mean to shout.'

'What? Oh, it's fine,' I muttered, my mind racing. 'Do they know how she died?'

He shook his head. 'That's the problem. Some reporter

at the scene announced that there was no obvious fatal injury, no blood or bruises —'

'So they're saying it's Mia.'

'She would never do this.'

I reached over and squeezed his hand. 'It sounds as though they don't know what happened —'

'I know, but Mia is not some —' He hesitated, started again. 'We don't even know exactly what she —'

He stared at me with pleading eyes and a heavy coldness seeped through me. 'Johan —'

'What if someone else was there that day on the island? What if there was a mistake, what if Mia did not —'

'There wasn't,' I said quietly. The pain in his eyes tore at me. 'There was just the three of us. She attacked you. She killed all those people, Johan. Sanna. Liv. Your —'

He flinched, and I broke off. Just before she disappeared, Mia hinted at luring Johan's father, in an alcoholic haze, to his death on the motorway that ran beneath the island. She had been seven years old.

'I'm so sorry,' I said. I held his hand in mine and stroked his fingers with my thumb. 'But I don't think it's helpful to —'

'I just think we cannot be certain of anything until she is found. Innocent until proven guilty, right?' His face twisted into a bitter grin and my heart lurched for him. They had been friends for over twenty years. This was killing him.

'Of course, but just —' How could I tell him not to get his hopes up? 'Has the counselling not helped you to recover any memories?' I said. Mia had attacked Johan, but he had been concussed.

'I remember finding Liv,' he said, his voice dull. He took a shaky breath, toyed with a forkful of stew. 'Then nothing until I woke up in hospital. Liv was her friend. It doesn't make sense.'

I reached over and took his hand in mine. 'No, it doesn't make sense. Nothing like that ever could. What Mia is — it's not supposed to make sense.'

'Maybe if I could remember her saying it —' He pulled his hand away, touched the hairline just above his temple. The scar where Mia had hit him with the blunt end of an axe glowed white. He caught me looking and moved his hand away.

THE AIR TAKES on an odd quality in deepest winter. It's simultaneously sharp with a bitter chill, and yet sort of thick, like an invisible fog. It's as though the cold gives it form. You can feel yourself breathing in a physical thing that coats the back of your throat and makes your nostrils stick together.

It hadn't actually snowed since yesterday morning, so most of the pavement I crossed on my way home was trampled into a treacherous hard sheet, packed several inches above the actual concrete. After skidding about eighteen times, I took to walking along the far edge, stamping through a thin crust of ice into the powdery snow beneath. My boots were quickly soaked through, but my neck would remained intact, so I considered the walk a success.

I never thought there could be such a thing as a flat smaller than Johan's, but I had found it. At least his has a separate sit-in kitchen and a sleeping alcove; mine was nothing but a single room with a teensy kitchenette I can barely stand in, never mind sit. The bathroom was so minuscule that washing my hair regularly left me with bruised elbows. Once, the morning after a night out with

Maddie and Lena I had even sat on the toilet to shower and it had worked admirably well. It's a good thing I don't have a great deal of space to fill, because I don't have a great deal of stuff. Or even a deal of stuff.

The sum total of my possessions was more or less the couple of suitcases full of clothes and knickknacks I brought to live at Johan's, plus a blow up mattress Maddie and Lena lent me. As luck would have it, the mattress all but fills the living area of the flat, and the bed side table I fashioned out of a cardboard box only sags and topples the lamp to the ground four or five times a night.

It wasn't not as weird as it sounds. I was simply being practical. The place was just a sublet while the woman who owns it worked, ironically enough, in London for a few months. By the time her secondment was over, Johan and I would be properly back on track, so buying a load of furniture would have been a waste of money and effort. I hadn't moved out, officially, I even still had a few things at Johan's. And we certainly hadn't broken up. It was just, breathing space.

I'd been insanely lucky to find it, in fact. There's this mad situation in Stockholm where there isn't really a private rental market. You can either be on a waiting list to rent from the city, but, as people take an almost weird amount of glee in telling you, the waiting list is about fifteen years long. So the only option is to semi-legally sublet from people who are working abroad or moving in with a partner, which means that opportunities to rent are like gold dust.

I'd sent out so many emails responding to ads that when I finally got the response saying I could have this place for a few months, I blinked at it for several seconds wondering if I was hallucinating. The fact that it was unfurnished explained why it hadn't been snapped up, but like most beggars, I had no other choice.

Maddie and Lena gave me their spare toaster which, let's face it, took care of most of my culinary needs. The weekend I moved in, I took an actual IKEA bus — which is a thing that exists and yes I was thrilled — out to the original IKEA and bought myself one cup, one spoon, one fork and so on, even including a little pot in case I decided to go wild and heat up some soup sometime.

I was quite fond of my weird little empty flat. Camping out in the middle of the city was an adventure. The perfect temporary solution.

I locked the door behind me and sat down on the floor to unlace my snow boots. My numb fingers slipped on the wet laces and my thumb jammed against one of the little metal thingies with a sharp shock of pain that brought tears to my eyes.

'Fuck it all to shit,' I shouted into the silence, then pressed my sore thumb to my mouth and leaned back against the wall.

3

'How on earth do you handle this cold?'

Kate Taylor shook her head as our coffees were served. She was the sort of brassy blonde that could drink a rugby team under the table and used terms like 'lovely jubbly' without a hint of irony. I'd been terrified of her sort at school, but within seconds of our arrival she'd regaled me with such a gloriously lurid tale of her encounter with a handsome Swede the night before that I quite liked her.

'Sorry darling, horrendously unprofessional,' she'd shrugged, 'but I was going to burst if I had to keep it in a moment longer, I'm still feeling the after shocks. They're awfully good at it, aren't they? Suppose one must keep warm somehow. What is it, minus fifty or something?'

'Welcome to Sweden,' I grinned, raising my coffee cup to hers.

She clinked and took a gulp, then grimaced. 'Good god, that'll put hairs on your chest. It's like tar. Glorious.'

We were in one of the oldest coffee shops in the city, over in Östermalm. Its entrance was tucked away in a courtyard off a side street and it was spread over several small rooms on two floors, each decorated like a little old lady's front room. We were sitting by a fireplace, in low, embroidered arm chairs, sipping from dainty china cups. If it hadn't been for the graphic sex story I'd just heard, I'd have felt as though we were a couple of little girls playing at having a tea party.

'I would say you get used to the cold,' I said, 'but I'd be lying. It hasn't gone above zero in about six weeks, and I can't remember the last time I was outside without having an ice cream headache from breathing. My boyfriend said that this year has been particularly harsh, but I'm beginning to understand why they all got a bit twitchy in September.'

'This is your first winter in Sweden?'

I nodded. 'I just moved over last —' I hesitated, though Kate knew perfectly well what had happened last summer.

'Quite, of course,' said Kate, putting her coffee cup down and wiping some cake crumbs from her mouth. 'Bother, have I ruined my lipstick? No matter,' she continued when I shook my head, 'I'm a complete wreck after last night in any case. Better sort myself out at the airport, bloody husband is picking me up at Heathrow.' She rolled her eyes. 'So. Your book.'

'My book?' I repeated dumbly.

Kate was from a small independent publisher in London. She had emailed me a couple of days ago to ask if we could meet when she was in Stockholm. My heart sank a bit. She appeared to have confused me with someone who had written a book.

'The book you're going to write for us,' she clarified with a grin. 'I've been reading your clippings, Ellie. They're good. Properly good. True crime is all the rage, and a first hand account of an encounter with a serial killer will sell like the proverbial. Chuck in the Scandi noir angle and it is a bloody genius plan all round, if I do say so myself.'

'But — but Mia hasn't been caught. She hasn't even been charged.'

'Yes, why is that?' Kate asked. 'From what I've managed to read she's bang to rights, is she not?'

I nodded slowly. 'She is. As far as I'm concerned. I mean, I was right there, I heard her confess.'

'Your boyfriend was there too, wasn't he?'

My stomach gave a little twist. 'He was quite badly injured so doesn't have any clear memory of it.'

Kate pursed her lips. 'But they found her lab on the island?'

Mia injected her victims with some sort of drug she had developed that caused instant catastrophic heart attacks.

'They did. But the problem is there isn't any direct evidence that links the lab to any of the victims, not least because they still don't know what it is she injects them with. There are no tests for drugs that don't officially exist.'

'Quite the pickle,' Kate murmured, chewing thoughtfully.

'So it's all circumstantial. She could claim she's simply a keen amateur scientist— if they ever find her to question her, that is. That's why they haven't charged her. Under Swedish law, a person can't be charged with a crime until they have been questioned.'

'Of course, I read something about that. So she can't be charged unless they find her.'

'And she seems to have disappeared into thin air. There are ships are going in and out of Stockholm to the Baltic States and Russia all day long, or she could have got hold of a car, driven over the bridge to Denmark. She could be anywhere in the world by now.'

Kate took a sip of her coffee, mulling this over. It was toasty next to the fire and the small window to my right was steamed up, but my toes in my snow boots were still icy. Even as I objected, I couldn't help the tiny flutter of excitement that had taken root in my stomach. *Ellie James, author.* I didn't hate the sound of that.

'There's still a story,' Kate said finally, and my heart leapt about three feet in the air. 'Even before she is caught. Perhaps her being still at large even gives it an extra frisson. She could strike again at any moment, after all. It could be something,' she added, nodding firmly. 'It definitely could. If you're in.'

A LITTLE WHILE later I sat on the bus watching the city trundle by. The sky was clear and the snow glowed pink in the afternoon twilight. I felt my phone buzz and looked down to see a text from Johan. *I had the weirdest dream we moved to a desert island and had a squirrel for a pet. We should do that. I love you xx*

I couldn't write a book about Mia. A cold, heavy feeling draped itself over me. Johan would never forgive me.

4

'Yeah, you know. Everything's fine. Not much to report.'

A few days later, I was sitting by the window of one of my favourite coffee shops, tucking into a cheese scone as I chatted to my mum on the phone. It had started to snow again that afternoon and fresh powder was dusted like icing sugar over the grey ice covering the cobblestones Outside, a guy in neon high-visibility gear struggled to control his bike over a patch of ice, and I wondered what possessed a person who is clearly concerned about safety to cycle down a steep hill in the snow.

'I just don't know what she's thinking getting a dog at her age,' my mum announced. 'I told her she'd regret it.'

Sue was my mum's neighbour, soul sister and favourite adversary. We'd lived next door to her since I was a baby, in a quiet little road of cramped terraced houses in Wandsworth. On the day we moved in mum drove up in her little Mini — a proper old school teeny one, not those giant ones they make now. I was in my car seat in the back and before Mum could even open the door, Sue poked her head in the passenger window and told her I was strapped in wrong. Mum was so stressed by all the packing and negotiating cramped little London roads with the moving van following close behind that she leaned over and punched Sue on the nose. Sue burst out laughing and announced she was babysitting me for the day so mum could unpack in peace.

'What's she even going to do with a dog?'

'I don't know,' I said, scraping the last of the cheese onto a bit of scone. 'Throw balls for it? Dress it up in little outfits? Whatever people do with dogs.'

'She'll regret it when it's raining and she's got to take it out.'

'I'm sure you'll be there to remind her,' I grinned. Mum sniffed. I could hear her banging around the kitchen as usual and I knew that the minute the dog arrived Mum would fall deeply in love with it and spoil it rotten forevermore.

I yawned. One of the many downsides of it getting full dark by mid afternoon is that your body clock starts feeling fairly confident it's bedtime long before dinner. For the first couple of weeks of December when the darkness properly rolled in, I'd felt permanently groggy, almost jet lagged. I'm almost certain I dropped off for a few seconds and snored in a coffee shop at least once. I now understood why the light of summer is celebrated with such passion.

'And Johan? Is he alright?' I'd brought Johan home for Christmas and he and mum bonded over her precious collection of recipe books. She'd not been his biggest fan before, on account of him being the reason I no longer lived around the corner from her in South London. They'd debated the best way to get the perfect roast turkey for hours on end while I zonked out in front of Christmas telly, and now he was apparently her dream son-in-law.

I hadn't mentioned the moving out bit. It was so temporary it wasn't worth the hassle of trying to explain.

'Yeah, he's — you know.'

'I know, love. He will be himself again in time. When your grandad passed I couldn't ever imagine smiling again, but you do.'

'It's not just that's he's grieving Liv,' I reminded her. 'Its everything with Mia as well, plus worrying about Krister. It's complicated.'

'Grief is grief, my love. And life goes on no matter what it throws at you.'

'I suppose.'

'Just being there is the main thing. I know you wish there was a magic wand you could wave to make everything all better for him, but there's not. I bet you're helping him more than you realise.'

It wasn't quite as simple as that. Johan wouldn't be in the pain he was were it not for me. That was the inescapable truth that had burrowed its way between us.

If I'd never met Johan, if I'd left him as a holiday fling, a lovely little memory of a few precious weeks in Thailand to keep me company during my dreary commute through London, Liv would probably still be alive. That wasn't guilt, it was just how it was.

'I'm starting a new job, actually,' I blurted.

'Oh yes? On one of the papers over there?'

'I can hardly write in Swedish, can I?' My voice came out a bit sharper than I'd intended.

'I know, I just thought maybe —'

'Remember my friend Maddie, the Australian? Well, some friend of a friend of hers runs a nursery school and they are desperate for assistant teachers. The school runs half in English to give the kids a head start with their second language, so they're keen on an English speaker. It'll be fun.'

'A nursery school teacher?' Mum said dubiously. 'Do you know anything about children?'

'It won't be forever or anything, just to get me on my feet a bit. Nice to have some regular money coming in and all that.'

It wasn't just the money. The idea of a bit of normality, routine, security, was so tempting I'd nearly bit Lena's hand off when she suggested it. A book deal wouldn't give me that, I'd reminded myself. Having somewhere to go every day, yawning on the bus in rush hour traffic, counting down the days til the weekend, that was the ticket. Eight hours a day during which I couldn't think about Johan or Mia or Liv. Maybe even getting to know a few of the teachers, getting together for the odd drink after work.

When you only know about five people in an entire country, the fact that one of them tried to murder you puts a serious dent into your social life. I was pretty confident I could sing a few rounds of The Wheels on the Bus for that. I could absolutely do it. It would all be fine.

5

This morning I woke up and I thought she was there. For just a few seconds, when I was in that hazy half-state between waking and sleep, I was so sure I felt her warmth next to me. I could hear her breathing softly in the darkness.

She was always such a silent sleeper. Not that I had many other women to compare her to, but when I'd shared a bedroom with my brothers, or with friends on camping trips, the air had been filled with snores and grunts and farts all night long. The first time I shared a bed with her, I had almost woken her in the night to check she was still alive.

The next morning I had told her that. I joked that I'd been tempted to find a little mirror to stick under her nose to make sure she was still breathing. She burst out laughing and said if she had woken up to a reflection of her own face at the end of her nose she would have had nightmares for the rest of her life.

She always had such a sense of humour. Biting, sometimes. She could be viciously funny about our friends, her colleagues, even my family, when she got going. I would always start out a little bit disapproving, insist that the person's heart was in the *right place and that we shouldn't judge. Seconds later I would be giggling helplessly alongside her. She got me every time.*

When I was a kid, I used to think that having a girlfriend was all about following rules, getting yelled for doing anything you wanted to do, like watching football or going out with your friends. 'Never get attached to a woman,' my dad would tell me, shaking his head wearily as his current girlfriend berated him for something or other.

He never took his own advice. By the time I was eleven or twelve I had given up bothering to learn any of their names. Dad would bring them home to meet us and my brother would ask if we should call her 'mother' just for the fun of watching them squirm, but I never did. I felt sorry for them, this endless procession of females who were all under the impression that their lives would be improved by spending time with my old man.

Our mother never had anyone else after him. I wondered about that sometimes, but when I asked her she just laughed and said that her friends and us boys were all she needed.

Being with her was nothing like I thought it would be. It was amazing. She never nagged me or gave me orders or stopped me from doing anything I wanted to. Most of the time we did the things she enjoyed, but that was just because we were so similar that I was happy to do them too. We had so much in common, and I didn't really want to spend my time with anyone else.

At least, that's how it was in the beginning, but all couples have their rocky times, don't they? Once, during one of our fights, one of the neighbours knocked on the door to ask if we were okay, and when he was gone we laughed and laughed. The idea that we didn't love each other desperately was nuts. We decided he was a moron and we laughed so much we forgot what we were arguing about. She was so sweet and loving that night that I almost wanted to thank the neighbour the next time I saw him.

And now I don't know what to do with myself any more.

There is so much time, so many hours in the day. I'm sure I remember being busy from the moment I woke until I fell in to bed at night. I would go for a morning run, shower quickly then head to work and talk to people all day long, then dinner with her. There was no time to think, to remember, to question everything I knew or thought I knew.

The only thing that fills me is memories. My life as it was then. Sometimes I think that maybe this is okay. That if living in the past in my head makes me happy, then what's the problem? As long as I still function, pay bills, talk to people, sleep, eat, exercise, then what happens inside my head is no one's business.

Maybe I was never busy and I've just forgotten. Everything is so foggy these days, I can't quite tell what's a memory and what was only ever my imagination. Maybe none of it was ever real. Maybe she never even existed.

6

The screaming. The screaming drilled into my bones and haunted my dreams. Even when it stopped for a moment I could still hear the echo ringing in my ears, reverberating through my skull.

How long until his parents came back?

'His name means thunder bear,' his dad had said ruefully that morning, as he tried to peel the red-faced, roaring child from around his knees. Tor-Björn had a mop of wild ginger curls and wore purple leggings and a jumper with a truck outlined in glitter. The dad, Casey, was American and a bit chattier than I could be arsed with. 'We didn't realise he'd take the name as a suggestion. My mom had some native on her side of the family, so I guess I should have realised. I guess we'll never lose him on a dark night.'

'Fab, so we'll see you in about an hour and a half?'

The Swedish schooling-in process meant that a parent spent the first couple of mornings at school with the kid, then left them for an hour or so, then a full morning, and so on. The past couple of days trying to bond with a wild two year old while making awkward conversation with Casey, who was the type that once you made eye contact with him he wasn't letting go until he told you his life story, had been bordering on excruciating. I'm sure Casey was lovely and all, but I probably hadn't needed to know how loved he'd been in high school.

He had recognised me from the little flurry of media that there had been about Mia and unfortunately appeared to be a bit of a true crime geek and wanted to know all about it. It wasn't my favourite subject at the best of times, and I was decidedly even less keen to discuss it whilst trying to engage a toddler in building blocks. Plus, I hadn't exactly mentioned my little side gig of catching serial killers whilst applying to work with small children, and my boss Sandra had overheard and pulled me to one side. That was an awkward conversation that let's just say hadn't exactly endeared me to Casey.

All that said, *come back Casey, all is forgiven*. It was mid morning and Tor-Björn's screams had been ringing in my ears since approximately the beginning of time. If it carried on much longer, I was likely to join him.

Sandra had given me a registration pack filled with information I was supposed to use to make him feel familiar and secure during this transition into nursery school. He always slept with a stuffed frog called *Koack*, his favourite song was apparently *Go Your Own Way* by Fleetwood Mac and he loved something called *pyttipanna*.

I'd tried *ribbeting* like a frog, I'd tried singing as much as I could remember of *Go Your Own Way*. I didn't know what *pyttipanna* was. He was apparently happiest at *mormor* and *morfar's* summer cottage on some unpronounceable island, but I had no idea how to incorporate that particular detail at the present time.

Tor-Björn was flung on a red bean bag by the reading

corner, yelling his head off. I was sitting cross-legged in front of him, awkwardly muttering 'there, there' every once in a while. Sandra, the senior teacher on our team, had the other kids gathered at the other end of the classroom, singing songs over the din. Every once in a while she would glance over to check on Tor-Björn and me. I'd wave to convey I was more than ready to admit defeat, and she'd give me a thumbs up and announce the next song.

Sandra was in her sixties and had been working at the school for almost forty years. 'When I started work we still told little boys they shouldn't cry,' she'd smiled as she showed me around on my first day. 'The newspapers like to make a lot of controversy about gender neutrality, but all we do is let children be themselves. If a little girl wants to play with dollies and glitter that is absolutely fine, and if a little boy wants to play with dollies and glitter that is also fine. The children let us know what they like to do.'

Her hair was wound in a long grey plait around her head like a milkmaid and she wore a brightly coloured, flowy caftan over leggings and rubber clogs. I was almost certain that I hadn't seen her repeat a caftan yet and I strangely envied her seemingly endless supply of wafty dress-things though not nearly as much as I envied her unflappable manner with the kids. She was like a flowy, Swedish, Mary Poppins, and I was like the hapless dad in a laundry detergent advert. In my first week I'd managed to put two nappies on back to front, leading to one fairly spectacular accident Sandra cheerily dubbed the 'festival of poo,' and clunked heads with a gigantic two year old so hard that I saw stars for the rest of the day.

'Look, look!' I shouted in desperation. 'What's this?'

Tor-Björn stopped crying and looked up with interest. I

scrabbled for the first thing that came to hand, which was a wooden building block. Excellent.

'Woooo,' I screeched in mild hysteria. 'I'm a building block and I'm flying! That's crazy! How can a block fly?'

I made the building block fly around Tor-Björn's head, zooming in to bop his nose now and then. For one glorious instant I thought I saw a flicker of a smile before his face crumped and the howls returned.

'Please, kiddo,' I muttered, feeling flutters of actual terror, 'I'll do anything. What do you want? Money? I will literally pay you to stop crying.'

This had little effect, which wasn't overly surprising given that he wasn't yet two and money meant nothing to him.

A bad thought occurred to me then. A forbidden thought.

I could give him his dummy.

Sandra had a strict dummies-are-for-naptimes-only policy. 'Keeping the spread of colds and other diseases to a minimum is difficult enough without them trading pacifiers all day, and they will,' she had explained. 'Plus a little incentive to lure them into the nap room comes in very useful.'

All good and sensible reasons. I quite agreed.

But Sandra was trusting me to handle the situation. It just so happened that my way of handling the situation involved handing over the magic plug of silence. I was taking an executive decision to comfort a child. More importantly, Sandra was all the way over at the other side of the classroom. She'd never even see.

'Hey kid,' I hissed, like a drug dealer outside a high school in a cautionary TV movie. '*Nappan?*'

At the magic word he looked up and we met one another's eyes in a silent agreement of collusion, although not silent, because one of us was roaring in anguish and the other one was also, albeit on the inside. I could see Tor-Björn's lime green dummy in its shiny new case on the shelf. I glanced over at Sandra but she was busy getting the kids to be trees on a windy day. The coast was clear.

Quick as a flash I darted to the shelf, grabbed the contraband and the silence was instant and blessed. Tor-Björn stared at me with placid eyes as I leaned on the bean bag next to him and started to read a story. Out of the corner of my eye I saw Sandra's triumphant wave of congratulations and I hardly felt guilty at all.

THAT EVENING, some sort of tinned concoction that appeared to be the Swedish answer to spaghetti hoops burbled away in my little pot. I leaned against my kitchen counter, my knees nearly touching the fridge opposite, scrolling idly through my phone. Some photos popped up from a female journalists' night out in London, a semi-regular get-together I had started a few years ago.

I was pleased it was carrying on without me. I had created something that lasted, that was something to be proud of. I was glad they looked as though they'd had a good time. It would be absurd of me to feel left out. But as I looked at the pictures of my old life, my friends making faces for the camera, miming glugging a full wine bottle, the inevitable theft of a traffic cone on the way to the night bus, a wave of something I didn't care to identify washed over me.

The life I'd left behind peered out at me from my phone. They would have spent the day badgering defence barristers coming out the Old Bailey, phone-bashing to track down elusive witnesses, triumphantly filing copy at the last second. After I'd been ticked off for the dummy incident, I'd taken another little boy, newly potty trained, to the toilet, forgotten to remind him to point down and he'd peed in my face.

I was on a brilliant adventure, obviously. I lived in Sweden, how cool was that? I had been completely prepared for some bumps along the way to settling in, it would have been ridiculous to have imagined otherwise. Obviously, I hadn't anticipated one of those bumps being a serial killer, but it was what it was.

The smell of burning finally pierced my consciousness and I discovered that I had managed to burn synthetic pasta shapes in fake tomato sauce. Only I could ruin food that wasn't even bloody real food. With an exasperated sigh I dumped the whole lot in the bin, yanked on eighty-seven thousand layers and headed to the pizza place around the corner.

'*Inte parmesan. Nej parmesan*,' I pleaded pathetically, and the pizza guy stared at me as though I had two heads. I have nothing against parmesan as a general rule, it's just that for whatever reason they pile so much on pizzas here it's all you can taste. It's fair to say that the pizza experience in Sweden an acquired taste. They come with something called pizza salad, which is sort of like a pickled coleslaw. It isn't bad but it doesn't remotely go with pizza. Further, I'm frankly embarrassed to admit that I live in a country where people consider banana an acceptable pizza topping. It is an abomination and one of these days I will confront the people of Sweden about it. Just as soon as I can speak more than a pitiable few words of their language.

I knew the word for 'without.' I'd looked it up after a particularly tragic incident in which I'd ended up screeching 'parmesan - NO' while making fairly undignified expressions of disgust. *Aldrig parmesan*? No, that wasn't it.

I'd lived in Sweden for almost eight months. I wouldn't expect to be effortlessly fluent by now exactly, but I was pretty horrified by just how crap I had turned out to be at remembering even the most basic phrases. I'd had all sorts of grand plans for watching TV and listening to the radio in Swedish every evening so as to immerse myself and intensify all the studying I fondly imagined I would do. Most nights, however, I was so drained by the time I got home that I'd collapse on my air bed craving the familiarity of mindless British soaps and comedy I wouldn't be caught dead watching at home.

Still, tomorrow was another day. I'd set my alarm early, I promised myself, and study a whole chapter of my Swedish vocabulary book before work. Starting with the bloody word for 'without.'

'*Fem minuter*,' said the pizza guy, which even I could gather meant 'five minutes.'

I sat on one of the little stools by the window. The window was steamed up, cutting us off from the world beyond. A group of twenty-something friends came in and loudly debated their pizza orders. A few of them wore the green, white and yellow scarves of Johan's football team — that explained why he hadn't texted me this evening, then. There must be a game on, he'd be watching with Krister. I can't bear football. I wouldn't have been interested even if he had invited me.

I pulled out my phone so that I didn't look too much like *the Little Matchgirl* staring enviously at a group of friends mucking about. I could message someone from home, I thought, opening my text app. One of the girls from the journalists' night out, surely there would be some gossip.

A news alert flashed up. They had identified the murder victim found at Mariatorget. Anna Essen.

It had nothing to do with me, I told myself firmly. I had done enough damage. I wasn't a journalist at the present time. I was a nursery school classroom assistant. Primarily a pee-soaked dummy enabler, but still. I should open up my Swedish language app and get in a bit of studying while I waited for my pizza.

I clicked on the news alert.

Minutes later, I'd picked my way through the dozens of articles about the murder. It just an opportunity to practice my Swedish. The guy behind the counter shouted over to me at one point, and I'd vaguely discerned from context and mime that my pizza was going to take a bit longer than five minutes.

Anna Essen had been one of those people whose career makes me feel old. She was a social media star, an influencer who seemed to earn a pretty hefty living simply by existing as a fabulous person and taking pictures of it. I had a peek at her Instagram, and there she was nibbling croissants in Paris, raising a champagne glass in a VIP tent at Coachella, attending a formal wedding of some minor royalty in Denmark.

Despite the ostentatious lifestyle on display, there seemed to be something genuine about her, I thought sadly, scrolling through her feed. She had an impish grin, in contrast with that weird cheekbones-sucked-in expression that minor celebs of her ilk seem to favour, and in loads of her photos she was crossing her eyes, caught mid giggle, squishing her face close to a friend's in a way that suggested genuine affection. I felt a wave of unbearable sadness as I watched a boomerang video of her twirling in a sparkly party dress, making a funny face at the camera.

She would have moved in similar circles as Mia and also Sanna, Johan's ex and one of Mia's most recent victims. Stockholm wasn't a big city and all the fancy people seemed to cross one another's paths sooner or later. The pizza place door opened, letting in a blast of freezing air, as I thought this over.

One of the reasons that Mia's trail of horror had gone undetected for so long was that the majority of her victims were people whose deaths rated a mention on page three or five at most. That sounds horrendous and I make no excuses for it, but the business of selling papers is what it is. Mia knew how it worked, and I believe she took advantage of it. Choosing a victim with a high profile, posing her like that in the middle of a busy square, it screamed for attention.

'*Hallå där? Din pizza?*'

I looked up and realised that my pizza had been sitting on the counter for goodness knows how long. I grabbed it with an apologetic smile and braced myself for the cold, my mind racing.

It wasn't until I got home and tucked into my stone-cold pizza, liberally strewn with parmesan, that I remembered. *Utan parmesan*. Bugger.

7

Mattias Eklund looked at himself in the mirror and immediately took his shirt off. The blue and white check was all wrong, he decided, he looked like a high school maths teacher. Not that there was anything wrong with being a high school maths teacher, it just wasn't the ideal look for a date.

Date. A wave of nerves rose up in Mattias's stomach and for a moment he thought he was going to be sick. He sat on the toilet seat and took a few deep breaths with his eyes closed. The nausea passed, but the nerves didn't. He was going on a date. His first date in Stockholm.

The plain dark blue shirt, he decided, pulling out of his closet. Mamma always said it brought out the colour of his eyes and made him look very handsome. He wasn't entirely sure that handsome by his mum's standards would cut it in Stockholm, but as it was the best he could realistically hope for at the present time, it would have to do.

The shirt collar was a bit crumpled, so he plugged in the iron and wondered if he should have got a haircut this afternoon. It wouldn't have made all that much difference.

Mattias often looked at the Stockholm men on the bus on his way to work, and wondered how they got their hair to be so slick and neatly combed. Mattias's hair was thick and poker straight yet always stuck stubbornly in a hundred different directions in a sort of fluffy mess.

He guessed there must be some sort of product that would control it, but he didn't know how to find out which one. In the tiny town he came from, in the middle of nowhere not far from the Norwegian border, if he ever saw a man with tidy, glossy hair, he would just go up to him and ask how he'd manage it. But he had never seen a tidy, glossy man at home, and he suspected it wasn't the done thing in Stockholm to tap somebody on the shoulder on the bus and ask them how they did their hair.

As he ironed, the familiar task soothing the nerves still churning in his stomach, he comforted himself with the thought that Camilla had already seen pictures of him with his hair on the dating app and had agreed to meet him. Against the advice of his more worldly cousin Jonas, Mattias had decided to upload a profile picture of his hair at its fluffiest — Jonas said it looked like a broom and a baby chicken had had a baby on his head — so that women would know what they were letting themselves in for. He didn't see the point in fooling anyone.

He wanted to meet a woman who knew exactly what he looked like, funny nose that was too big, oddly pointy shoulders and ridiculous hair, and for her to want him anyway. Jonas had rolled his eyes and predicted that Mattias wouldn't get any matches, but he was wrong. Camilla had matched him the first day — Mattias had almost dropped his phone in shock — and even though she was nothing less than breathtakingly beautiful in Mattias's opinion, she replied to his message. They had texted back and forth for more than three weeks now, sometimes late in to the night, sharing childhood stories and secret fears.

A small part of Mattias was afraid it would turn out to be a prank, that he would arrive for the date to meet a bunch of the hockey guys from his school, all doubled over with laughter that broom-head Mattias thought a girl liked him. That was the reason he refused the first time Camilla suggested meeting. He'd claimed he just wanted to get to know her through text a bit better first, though in truth he thought he might explode if he existed another minute without seeing her in real life. Every night, he fell asleep imagining the sound of her laugh, the smell of her hair, the softness of her skin he would discover if he got to touch her hand.

Even though she had agreed to keep texting for a bit longer, Mattias had worried and worried that she was hurt, so after a sleepless night he had texted her at five the next morning confessing the truth. She had replied with three whole lines of laughing emojis and promised she was not a hockey team. Then she suggested she phone him so that he could hear her voice and know that she was at least a woman.

They had talked for three hours and when they hung up, Mattias admitted to himself that he was in love,

Now, he was going to meet her for the very first time and if he didn't put his shirt on and go, he would be late. He nearly dropped the iron in horror as he pictured her sitting at the pub alone, anxiously watching the door and thinking he hadn't shown up. Over the phone, she had confessed that she had been stood up by the first date she arranged through the app, and would never know whether the guy had decided not to come, or if he had taken one look at her and left. Cold chills cascaded over Mattias at the thought he might make her think that.

He laced up his snow boots so quickly that he got the laces in all the wrong holes, and after checking three times he had unplugged the iron, he stepped out into the night. The chill hit his face and he dug his hands deep into his pockets as sheer thrill exploded in his stomach like a firework and pins and needles zapped through his whole body. He was about to meet her. Maybe, just a couple of short hours from now, he would get to kiss her. His whole life was about to start.

8

A murder victim had been found posed, standing, frozen, in a park in Boston six years ago. My mind was whirring as I ran alongside the canal that separates Söder from Hammarby to the south. The temperature was about minus a billion and every time I breathed in I got an ice cream headache. The snow that had fallen all afternoon lay soft and innocent looking on top of treacherous layers of ice.

I could hear the big ice breaker machine working a few blocks away. It's a bit like a normal street cleaner, except with this gigantic hammer-thing at the front which smashes up the several-inches thick layers of ice that cover roads and pavements, then sweeps them towards the gutter. During a heavy winter like this, every street is bordered by high piles of snow and ice, so that crossing the road can necessitate hopping over a muddy igloo wall.

Remind me why I'd chosen this bloody city to take up running in?

After wolfing down the parmesan-pizza the night before I'd given up pretending I wasn't interested and had been up most of night searching and scribbling and cross referencing. Sometime around four, I'd stumbled across this American case.

Posed like a statue, standing in the snow. It was too similar. Too weird and unique to be a coincidence.

The victim, Jason Winslow, had been a student at Boston University. He walked a date home to her dorm at Harvard and was never seen again. He was a young, handsome guy from what they referred to as an old Boston family, and he had played basketball for his college, so his murder had caused quite a media splash. The investigation had dominated the Massachusetts news for months on end, featuring breathless daily updates as more and more students were questioned, including even a minor Kennedy. Months went by, the case hit a few national papers, but absolutely zero leads were ever found and six years later it remained unsolved. Much was made of the sheer weirdness of the victim being found posed in a park alongside the Charles River, standing up in the snow, arms waving as though he were a politician addressing a rally or something.

I'd looked that up, wondering how it was even possible. I knew that bodies stiffened after death, but surely they would have to be posed while still pliable, and then — what? The killer stood there holding them still while rigor mortis set in? It put me in mind of gluing together crafty projects copied from kids' TV when I was little. I never had the patience to hold the lollipop sticks, or whatever it was, together long enough for the glue to set so as soon as I let go the whole thing would collapse.

It turned out that there was a thing known as extreme embalming. It was even a minor trend in the States. The body of a loved one would be injected with a chemical that froze their body like a statue, then posed in a chair in pride of place at the wake. I'd come across several deeply disturbing photos of families gathered around a suspiciously pale looking Granny, which looked to me the stuff of nightmares, but you know, whatever floats your boat.

No other signs of fatal injury had been found on Jason Winslow's body. The medical examiner had concluded it was impossible to tell whether or not he had been dead prior to the embalming process.

The sheer thought of being embalmed alive was so horrifying it took my breath away. He couldn't have been conscious, surely, when the blood was drained from his body and replaced with a chemical? It made me think of the old black and white vampire films I loved, except instead of fangs a clinical needle. When I'd come to the end of that article, about twenty minutes ago, I'd slammed shut my laptop and grabbed my running shoes.

It was quiet down by the canal, and the rhythm of my feet lulled me into an almost pleasant mindlessness. The lights of Hammarby twinkled in the distance and the thin sheet of ice covering the canal shimmered in the moonlight. Every morning the commuter ferry smashed its way through the ice and every evening the ice froze again, so there were layers of cracks and jagged edges that glittered when the sun finally rose mid morning, reminding me of a kaleidoscope I'd had as a child.

I should have skipped my evening run tonight, I thought as my throat burned with every breath. I hadn't felt my toes in several minutes. Being outdoors in this temperature was reckless, I chided myself as I slowed to a walk, rubbing the stitch in my side with a grimace.

If it hadn't been quite so painfully cold I would have walked right past him.

He was sitting on one of the benches that overlooked the

canal, hands clasped in his lap, head bent. If it had been a reasonable temperature I'd have assumed he was having a little think, or a snooze. Heaven knew I'd sat right where he was, catching my breath, many a time. But surely no one could sit still in this weather, I thought, hesitating a few metres away.

The bench was situated in between two street lamps, not quite close enough to either to benefit from the light, so I could barely make him out in the gloom. He was wearing a dark winter coat with a fur lined collar, a thickly knitted hat pulled low over his forehead and snow boots that reached half way up his shins. He was certainly dressed for the cold.

'Excuse me? *Ursäkta*? Are you okay?' I called, my voice thin and reedy in the glacial air. I glanced around, suddenly acutely conscious of the silence, the darkness. A bus rumbled in the distance, laughter pealed from a nearby balcony. I wasn't alone, I reminded myself as pins and needles nipped at my fingertips. If I screamed, I would be heard.

The moon slipped out from behind a cloud, bathing the figure in a silvery glow and I saw the blue sheen of his skin. *Oh he's dead*, I thought with a curious dullness. I probably should have noticed that in the first place.

He was one of them. Extreme embalmed to sit upright on the bench, watching boats chug along the canal for all eternity. My breath caught in my throat and I fumbled for my phone and dialled 112.

He was practically a boy, early twenties or so. Sadness seeped through me as I waited for the police. I couldn't get too close to him or risk contaminating the scene, but I wanted to be nearby. I wanted to keep him company. He was so young. Handsome, in a sweet, boy next door kind of way. His mum probably whispered loudly in delight every time she saw a girl checking him out. He would blush furiously and hiss at her to be quiet but secretly be thrilled and terrified.

Just as I heard the siren approaching in the distance I noticed a tiny cut on his neck where he had nicked himself shaving, and I burst into tears.

9

'Mattias Eklund,' said Henrik, the detective I always thought looked as though he fancied himself a retired rockstar. His hair was reached his shoulders and and was scraggly, peppered generously with grey and his leathery tan was more than a little suspicious in Sweden at this time of year. I hadn't exactly warmed to him when he and his partner Nadja questioned me with regards to a murder Mia had committed last summer, but now it was strangely comforting to see a familiar face.

He had just joined me in the backseat of the patrol car that was parked haphazardly across the tram tracks at the edge of the canal. He rubbed his hands together and blew on them to try to get some feeling back in them as I stared out the window at the Crime Scene in front of us.

A young uniformed officer, a woman with a long plait that reached down her back, had ushered me into the car as her partner stared at the victim, aghast. He looked green and I guessed he was regretting being the closest patrol car when I called. The female officer was tall and had a reassuringly no-nonsense air about her. I'd gratefully allowed her to march me across the ice to the car as my body shuddered with empty sobs.

'I've no idea why I'm crying,' I'd muttered as she covered my knees with a blanket from the boot. 'I didn't know him or anything. It's just so sad, he is so young.'

She nodded with that sharp intake of breath Swedes seem to think is a response, and closed the car door behind me. I'd sat there trapped until Henrik joined me a few moments ago. Though I was grateful for the warmth of the car — my skin tingled as feeling rushed back into it — I couldn't help but feel strangely guilty, locked in the back seat of a police car like a criminal.

The crime scene was buzzing with action, a white tent set up around the young man's body, Scene of Crime Officers in their white suits swarming, collecting, processing, analysing. Powerful floodlights illuminated the scene, punctuated every once in a while by a camera flash. The blue lights from several police cars rotated lazily, making the whole scene seem alien and surreal.

'Have you ever heard that name before?' Henrik asked me. 'Mattias Eklund. Did you recognise him?'

I shook my head. I'd never seen the young man's face before tonight, though now I couldn't get it out my head. They way he frowned as though in deep thought. Was that his own expression or had the killer arranged his face to suit their purpose?

'There is a thing called extreme embalming,' I said. I felt bone tired all of a sudden, as though I could happily slip in to a deep sleep then and there and never wake up.

'Yes we know.'

'Is that what happened to Anna Essen?'

'I am unable to share the details of the investigation with you.'

'There was a serial killer operating on this island for nearly fifteen years and you wouldn't even know she existed if it wasn't for me,' I snapped. 'Then you let her sail off into the night right under your bloody noses. And now here we are again. Two bodies in a couple of weeks. How many more before you catch this one?'

'None, we hope.'

I sighed. The door of the medical examiner's van was slammed shut and it began to crunch slowly over the snow. Someone shut down the crime scene lights and we were plunged into darkness.

'There was a body found in Boston six years ago,' I said. Henrik didn't respond, but opened his notebook and started to write. 'Standing up in a park, frozen. Extreme embalmed. They never found the killer.'

'Boston is a long way from Stockholm,' he murmured.

'Yeah they have these things called planes these days.'

'Do you think it's a coincidence that you found this victim?' Henrik asked.

A little chill trickled down my spine. 'Yes. Of course. It must be. What do you mean, what else could it be?'

'It is not the first dead body you have found in Stockholm.'

'Some of us have all the luck.'

'Do you run along this canal often?'

'Most nights,' I admitted.

'At about the same time?'

I shrugged.

'So anyone who was familiar with your routine might expect you to be here this evening?'

'Someone like Mia do you mean?' I asked, icicles slithering into my guts. The darkness beyond the lights of the crime scene suddenly seemed deeper. I pictured Mia standing there, shrouded in shadows, watching the commotion with a satisfied smirk.

'For example.'

Wasn't there a sighting of her in Italy last week?'

'That proved not to be credible,' Henrik replied stiffly. 'We have consulted a profiler who specialises in the psychological make-up of people like Mia,' he continued, after a moment.

I turned to look straight ahead at the headrest in front of me. There was a piece of duct tape holding one side of it together. I shuddered to think of who might have sat where I was now, slashing the back of the headrest.

'She was of the opinion that Mia has no reason to hide any more. She controlled herself to kill so subtly for so long that it must have caused a great deal of strain for her.'

'My heart bleeds.'

Henrik smiled. 'But now every person in the country knows her name. School children sing songs in the playground about her. We have been monitoring any so-called natural death in the area and there has not been one that raised even the slightest suspicion in all these months. This is not uncommon. Many killers go cold for months, even years, especially if they have been frightened by something. But, the profiler warned that it was only ever a pause. She predicted that Mia's next kill or kills would be —' He gestured vaguely.

'Show-offy,' I supplied, my heart hammering.

I tried to picture Mia carrying Mattias's body, placing him on the bench, arranging him to her satisfaction, imagining my horror when I ran past and saw him.

'This Jason Winslow, if he was a semi-professional basketball player, he would be a huge guy, wouldn't he? And Mattias Eklund was no short-arse either. Any corpse is pretty heavy, but guys of that size would weigh a ton. Mia's not a delicate flower but I don't think any woman could easily carry them.'

'That is true,' Henrik conceded. He nodded towards the bench, though we could barely see it any more. 'The killer kicked around the snow so there are no identifiable footprints, but there were no markings to indicate they staggered or dragged the body.'

'So maybe it was a coincidence I found him,' I said finally. 'Loads of people run down here, there's a bus stop just there.'

'Perhaps you should be careful anyway,' Henrik replied mildly. 'I will drive you home now.'

10

The flat was freezing when I got home, the cold seeping in through the walls themselves. I put on my beloved giraffe onesie, made a cup of tea and burrowed under the covers on my air mattress. I switched my lamp off and stared at the unrelenting blackness beyond the window.

Was Mia out there? Watching me? Following me?

I was so cold I felt my organs chill. I could picture them inside me, frosty and blue-tinged. A wave of sadness washed over me as I remembered Mattias Eklund, frozen on that bench. That poor kid. Had he died because Mia wanted revenge on me?

Little tingles of horror danced on the back of my neck. I wasn't to blame for Mia's actions. Of course I knew that. But there was no getting away from the fact that it was me who stumbled across Sanna's body. Mia had been safe until I came along.

Johan had described how they heard me screaming that night and had scrabbled from the table, come running through the forest. He had thought I'd hurt myself, but she must have known, must have suspected at least, what I had found, why I screamed. What had she been thinking?

I had taken on the investigation in the hopes of clearing Johan's name. I'd asked questions and uncovered clues and poked sleeping bears that made life uncomfortable for her. And when life was uncomfortable for Mia, it became dangerous for the rest of us.

A week or two ago, Johan had invited Krister and I over for dinner. As we ate, I'd told them a funny story about a little boy in my class who had taken to calling his parents by their first names for no apparent reason. A snack time, Sandra had refused him a third bowl of cereal and he'd dramatically thrown himself on the floor howling 'Karen would let me!' Johan and Krister had dutifully laughed. I stopped talking for a moment to take a bite, and the silence that descended was palpable.

Later that evening Krister laced up his snow boots while I hugged Johan goodbye. I went to kiss him on the cheek, but at the last second he turned for my lips and we ended up in an awkward head smash. Krister was already out in the hallway, and Johan pulled me back into a tight hug that brought a lump to my throat. I could feel his breath warm on the back of my neck as he burrowed his face in my shoulder, the contours of his back so achingly familiar as I stood on tip toe to hold him close. Maybe I should just stay. What harm could it do? Maybe he needed company, maybe —

'I guess you should go, before it gets too late,' he murmured into my hair.

For once I was grateful for Krister's silence as we rode the creaky lift down and I blinked back tears.

'These murders demand attention,' I had said to Henrik earlier this evening, when he pulled up outside the flat. 'The public places they are left out, the posing. There's nothing subtle about it. The killer is making a point.'

Henrik nodded. 'Yes, that is a good theory.' He turned the engine off and stared blankly as the car fell into silence. I watched his reflection in the windscreen, noticing for the first time how exhausted he looked. He had a little furrow in his brow that made him look as though he were permanently frowning.

'And if it's Mia, you think she could be making a point at me.'

'It is possible she blames you for — disrupting her life.'

'So you're saying I've got a serial killer willy waving at me,' I muttered. I opened the car door and a blast of freezing air smacked me in the face. 'Fucking brilliant.'

But as the tea finally started to defrost my insides and I felt sleep begin to wash over me, I found myself thinking about an evening, back in the summer, when we had all gone out for dinner. Me, Johan, Mia, Krister and Liv. I remembered how couldn't get over how utterly flawless Mia's makeup was, and remained throughout the meal.

There wasn't the tiniest clump of mascara on a single eyelash, her skin was porcelain-perfect, and her lipstick didn't smudge once. I should have known then, I thought with a rueful smile. Never trust a woman who can eat a burrito without mucking up her lipstick.

While Krister fell into sullen silence, Liv barely concealed her disdain for me and I talked a load of nonsense at a mile a minute in a desperate ploy to cover up the awkwardness, Mia was the ultimate hostess. She told stories, she asked questions, she listened to the answers with encouraging nods and unwavering eye contact. Looking back now, I could see that she was too perfect. We all say daft things that come out wrong sometimes, snort when we laugh, struggle to conceal our boredom or tiredness, but not Mia. Mia was flawless precisely because she wasn't real. She was a consummate actress playing the part of a human being.

And she had tremendous stamina for it. For well over a decade, she spent hours on end at social events, she lived with Krister, all the while keeping this secret. Never once did her mask slip, not even for an instant. Mia wasn't your run-of-the-mill criminal whose very lack of impulse control would get her caught sooner or later. She was highly functional, highly intelligent, highly determined. She had existed fully in a double life, coldly, capably covering her tracks completely She wouldn't have abandoned the MO that had served her for so long for a piddly thing like almost getting caught.

This killer, posing their victims in a showy display of ego, was a different beast. I was sure of it. It was risky, posing bodies in public like that. Foolhardy, even. *Look at me, look what I did.*

I braced the cold to scuttle out of bed to brush my teeth, then snuggled back under the covers on the air mattress. I was wide awake. I turned onto my back and stared at the ceiling, criss crossed with shadows from the streetlights outside.

Then a thought struck me.

It was last summer, the night Mia and I had shared a bottle of wine at a basement bar near Johan's flat. I'd been there to stalk Gustav Lindström, Sanna's ex boyfriend, who I'd thought at the time could have been responsible for her murder. Mia killed him later that night.

At some point during the evening, I'd told her a story about a trip to New York, years back, with some friends. One of our group had just broken her engagement, so we took her away for the weekend over Valentine's day to take her mind off things. I'd suggested New York, picturing a hard-nosed city full of wisecracking, take no prisoners types who'd shout colourful abuse at us for crossing the road in the wrong place. It turns out, however, that Americans take Valentine's day rather seriously and we had arrived to find Manhattan basically draped in love hearts and glitter. In desperation, we took her to an ice hockey game, and she was caught on the giant kiss-cam screen, sobbing her heart out as the couple in the row in front of us snogged each other's faces off.

'I should have known,' I'd grinned that night at the bar, shaking my head at the memory. 'Americans do have a *go big or go home* attitude to any holiday. I was in New Orleans once for Halloween, I'm not sure I've ever recovered.'

Mia shrugged. 'I wouldn't know, I've never been.'

'You've never been to the States, ever?'

She shook her head. 'I don't like to fly. Krister and I take trains around Europe every summer. We thought about taking a cruise to New York sometime, but I've never bothered to get a passport. I will someday.'

It was gone midnight, but Henrik answered on the first ring. 'Does Mia has a passport?'

'What?'

'Mia. She told me once she'd never got a passport. I remember it because I've never heard of anyone without a passport before. Was she lying?'

I heard a few clicks of the keyboard on the other end, a muffled yawn. 'No,' he said after a few moments, 'she wasn't. There is no passport registered in her name.'

'So she wasn't in Boston six years ago.'

There was a silence as Henrik took this in. 'No, I suppose she was not.'

We hung up, and before I could lose my nerve, I fired off an email to Kate, the publisher in London.

Developing case here. I just found one of the victims. Different killer. Interested in a new story?

Seconds later, the reply arrived. *Sounds glorious. Hooray and indeed hurrah.* '

I was back in business.

11

It was summer. She and her little sister Lisbet were playing in the garden of their grandparents summer cottage, while the adults finished a bottle of wine after lunch.

It was a beautiful day. If she were to close her eyes now, she could feel the sun on her face, the sting of sunburn on her shoulders and nose, the tug of the too-tight plaits Mamma insisted the girls wore their hair in at all times. She was seven years old and her dearest wish was to be able to wear her hair loose around her shoulders like a princess in a story book, but Mamma insisted it would get tangled and messy and she had no time for that.

She was standing in the water at the bottom of the garden, feeling sand and rocks beneath her toes, waves lapping gently around her ankles. Even though she had won three swimming medals at school, neither she nor Lisbet were permitted to paddle without an adult nearby, in case a freak current washed them out to sea.

She stepped further the water with a deliberate splash. Lisbet, playing nearby with a bucket and spade even though the beach was rocky so all you could do is fill the bucket with stones and tip them out again, gasped. Lisbet's eyes had widened and she had been about to say something, or worse, shout for Mamma.

'I'm not going in deep, anyway.' She was annoyed with herself. She didn't have to explain herself to her little sister. Lisbet was only four and didn't know anything except how to tattle and whine when she didn't get her way.

It made her laugh to remember how excited she had been to meet her new little sister. Her grandparents had driven her up to the hospital in their new car which was mint green and enormous. Even sitting in the front seat in between them, she could hardly see over the top of the walnut dashboard, but she felt very important and she liked that.

Then they arrived in the little room and Mamma was sat up in a narrow bed wearing the new peach dressing gown she had bought at PUB two weeks before. She didn't look like Mamma. She looked sort of puffed up and deflated at the same time. Mamma gave a tired smile but looked distracted, which was worrying.

Mamma held a squirming, mewling bundle in her arms.

The new big sister peered over to have a look. At first, she thought it was a cat, which would have been interesting. She was incensed to learn, however, that this tiny red-faced thing was the little sister she had been so looking forward to. 'I can't play with that,' she wailed, burying her face in Grandma's skirts. All the adults had laughed, which just made her even angrier.

Lisbet was now technically old enough to play with now, but she had never been forgiven for being such a disappointment.

Every time she remembered Grandma telling her off as

she dragged her down the hospital corridor away from Mamma, she would pinch Lisbet, sometimes hard enough to bruise her. Lisbet never told on her. She just gave her a wide-eyed stare full of hurt and shock, and didn't even cry.

Lisbet was pathetic.

That summer, the big sister was determined to learn how to skip a stone across the surface of the water. One day back in spring, she had been walking with Pappa when they came across some boys skipping stones. She wanted to join in with them, but when she tried, her stone just plopped into the water and sank immediately. The boys had laughed and Pappa tried to comfort her and she hated all of them.

She threw a flat pebble with a flick of her wrist, and it hit the water — and then immediately sank. She stamped her foot. She must have the wrong kind of stones. Pappa had collected some flat ones for her to practice with that morning. He promised they were ideal for skipping, but obviously he lied or was too stupid to know which kind of stones were right for skipping. Probably both.

She tried again with an even flatter stone. It hit the water, then — again! She'd done it. She had learned all by herself and she hadn't even had to wait for useless Pappa who had probably forgotten he promised to help.

'Well done!' shouted Lisbet from where she perched on the beach behind her. 'I knew you would do it eventually!'

Eventually? She had only been trying for about five minutes. Not even that, two minutes at most. There was no eventually about it. How dare this snivelling little idiot who still wet herself sometimes lie that it took her a long time to learn how to do something as stupid and easy as skipping stones.

She turned around with a smile. Lisbet grinned, then she must have seen something in her sister's eyes because her grin faded. She didn't move, just sat there staring like a frightened animal. She knew what was going to happen.

'Thank you, Lisbet,' she called, knowing that her voice would carry up to where the adults sat on the porch. Then she raised her arm and threw the stone right at Lisbet's head.

It hardly hurt her. It was tiny. All that screaming for nothing.

So there was a little bit of blood where it hit her eyebrow and Lisbet threw up and said she felt dizzy. She was fine. She was just crying because the adults were all fussing around her.

Her parents and grandparents came rushing across the garden when Lisbet screamed. Too late, it occurred to her she should have run over to Lisbet too, pretended to be all concerned like they did. But she was annoyed at Lisbet for screaming and making a fuss.

Later, she told Pappa she had been too frightened to move because she was afraid Lisbet was going to die. She heard him explaining this to Mamma when he thought she was asleep. Mamma seemed to be arguing with him. All the next day, Mamma kept stealing nasty little looks over at her elder daughter when she thought she wasn't looking.

So she was still standing in the water, far away from the little family group, when it happened. She saw it before she heard anything. Lisbet's fat little arm pointing, her face accusing, the four adults turning to stare at her.

'Of course I didn't!' she gasped. She wasn't even sure if any of them had said anything out loud, but she could see the accusation in their eyes. Her bottom lip started to wobble and her eyes filled with tears as she began to tremble with the horror, the injustice of all.

Lisbet had pointed at her. For the first time in four

whole years, Lisbet hadn't just stared in mute shock. She had tried to get her into trouble.

She was inconsolable. Pappa was the first to apologise, then her grandparents. Even Lisbet said she was sorry before Mamma did.

But she wasn't really upset by that point. She had just got quite used to crying and had forgotten to stop. She howled that she was sad and hurt, even after everyone apologised again, but she wasn't really sad and hurt. She was angry.

And, now, many years later, she was still angry. Lisbet died a long time ago. Mamma and Pappa went soon after her. Some people said they had died of broken hearts after burying their beautiful daughter so young. They didn't say out loud, but she knew they meant her parents didn't want to be left with the daughter who was distinctly un-beautiful, in every way. Her grandparents must have died at some point along the way, but she can't particularly remember. Her anger never died though, she has just learned to channel it in different directions.

12

'*Tre, två, ett... nu kör vi!*'

The instructor blew his whistle, turned up the pounding rap music and I punched Maddie. I'm sorry. I can't explain what I've become either. I blame Sweden. All that strapping outdoorsy fit keenness is as catching as the clap.

I'd just been leaving school that afternoon when Maddie texted, and suddenly enduring the horrors of some fight-bootcamp had seemed preferable to going straight home to think about serial killers. That said, whatever psychopath came up with the bright idea of forcing people to punch a boxing pad held by their partner then do untold number of burpees for the longest minute known to man I don't know, but should I meet them I know where I'll tell them where to stick their burpees.

'Come on Ellie, put some welly into it,' shouted Maddie over the music. She'd barely broken a sweat while I was fairly sure I'd broken my soul. Luckily for her I was unable to form a response, but I gave her a look I liked to think spoke volumes, and she smiled sweetly.

The instructor, a former cage fighter with a scarred face and cauliflower ears, held his baby son in a sling across his chest as he marched around the room yelling at people to go harder. The baby, wearing luminous green earphones, giggled delightedly at a woman slamming heavy battle ropes into the ground. The instructor blew his whistle again and announced a water break.

'So is this Ola Andersson guy credible, do you think?' Maddie asked as I slithered to the ground and squirted water over my face. 'Lena and I saw it on the news this morning.'

'Who?'

Maddie grabbed her phone, clicked to a news story and handed the phone to me. A guy with neatly combed, almost white blond hair and a little moustache that made him look a bit like a World War Two officer, was being led from a police car past a flurry of news cameras into a building. He stared into the lens as he passed by with a slight frown, as though he were mildly baffled by all the commotion. The headline identified him as Ola Andersson.

'He's accusing his ex girlfriend of the ice statue murders. That's what they're calling them.'

I clicked to play the video again, frowning as I tried to process it. 'He just walked into a police station and said 'I know who the killer is'?'

Maddie nodded. 'Seems that way. Weird that there were already a bunch of photographers there, but no one seems sure if he called them or if it was a police leak or something.'

I shook my head. The name Lotta Berglund flashed on the screen, accompanied by a photograph of a serious looking woman, her dark blonde hair tied neatly back. She wore wire-rimmed glasses and a plain white shirt and stared unwaveringly at the camera.

'It's not clear whether or not it's credible?' I asked.

Maddie shrugged. 'Lena said that the statement he made publicly was pretty vague, though he might have given more details to the police that are being kept secret, I guess.'

'It's a helluva thing to accuse someone of if you're not certain.'

'Yeah it's a weird one, that, isn't it?' said Maddie. A couple of guys at the next station were spending the break daring one another to deadlift the weight of a small car, or something.

'Lena and I talked about it after we met Krister when we all had dinner that time. On the one hand, your partner is the person who knows you best, so if anyone would know it would be them. On the other, they're also the one the most invested in you being a good person and we all know denial is a powerful thing. So two things that have to be true cancel one another out. How could they possibly have known and how could they possibly not have known.'

The instructor called out a five second warning and Maddie yanked me to my feet. I picked up the boxing pads for her turn with the punch-burpee routine, though withstanding her blows without falling over was as much as of a workout for me.

'So, I guess,' Maddie continued, not even out of breath, as she punched and nearly flung me against the wall, 'for this guy to get to a place where he would betray his girlfriend completely like this, he must be beyond certain, right?'

'Johan will be thrilled if it's true.'

'*Vatten!*' hollered the instructor. Water break.

'What do you mean?' Maddie took off the boxing gloves, wiped the slight sheen of sweat from her forehead with the back of her arm.

'From what Henrik said last night, it sounded as though the police are at least considering the possibility that the cases are all linked,' I said slowly, trying to piece it all together in my mind. 'If Lotta Bergland is the killer, then he'll be hoping it means Mia is innocent altogether.'

We walked to the next station, some torture-fest involving kettlebells.

'You don't think that, do you? You saw her whack Johan over the head.'

'I did, but he doesn't remember it.'

'But he knows it happened.'

'I don't know if he believes she is innocent exactly, as much as —' I shrugged, trying to find the words. 'It's like — you know when you've got to a place where you are over someone, but just in your head? You've thought it all through and realised that they aren't the person for you, you wouldn't even want them back — then something reminds you of them you burst into tears? Your head is there but your emotions haven't got the memo? I think it's something like that for Johan. He accepts on some intellectual level that it must be true, it's just not sunk in deep enough to stick.'

'I get that,' Maddie said thoughtfully. 'My family was pretty religious when I was a kid. Church every Sunday, grace before meals, prayers at bedtimes, the whole shebang. It was just what we did. As an adult, I haven't been to church in years and I don't really know what I believe any more, if anything. Lena always laughs if I describe myself as a Christian, but it would feel too weird to say otherwise, even though she's not wrong it probably isn't true any more. When you've believed in something for such a long time, it's pretty tough to shake.'

'Krister took back the statement he made about Mia,' I

said. 'Johan told me this morning. He didn't know anything about the murders, but after the island, when Johan was in hospital, he made a statement that described their relationship in a way that could have added domestic violence to the potential charges against her. Not physical, but coercion and control. Then a few weeks ago he phoned up the police and retracted it.'

'She's put a lot of conditioning in. Poor guy must be spinning.'

'I think they both are.'

The instructor approached to yell at me but Maddie waved him away. The baby squealed over the music and the instructor roared at someone else to *jobba*.

'What do you think?' she asked me again. 'About Mia.'

'I heard her say it, Maddie. She confessed. She laughed at me. She attacked Johan. I saw it with my own two eyes.' I sighed, trying to find the words.

'I don't have the history with her that Johan and Krister had, but I thought she was my friend. She was nice to me, I liked her. I never once suspected her. If anything,' I gave a slightly bitter smile, 'I'd have been less surprised if it turned out to be Liv. It's not as though I found out about her history with chemistry and the fact she was behind the rumours about Johan and went *oh yes of course*.

'I still struggle to wrap my head around the Mia I thought I knew with how she was that day on the island. Then she was just gone. The cottage was the fire, I thought I had lost Johan — then the police arrived and she had disappeared into thin air.

'Johan's boat was found a couple of days later, it had drifted into a narrow causeway between another couple of islands and got stuck on some rocks. There was no sign of her, no fingerprints on the boat, no nothing. It's just so surreal it sometimes feels as though I dreamt the whole thing.'

I took a shaky breath, thoughts tumbling around my brain. I kept picturing Mia wading into the water to greet me the first time I met her at Midsummer. Her arms were flung wide, her smile so open and welcoming. I remember the relief I felt that I had a friend, an ally. The night we shared a couple of bottles of wine at the bar with all the ping pong tables. Had she really hugged me goodbye then cold-bloodedly murdered Gustav Lindström an hour later?

'She said *I can't kill you, you're not one of the special ones*. I heard her say those words. I'm sure I did. Then she talked about the man in the tunnel, Johan's dad.'

'Those are the words you reported to the police?' Maddie asked.

I nodded. 'You wouldn't say *I can't kill you*, unless you'd killed other people. Right?'

'Definitely not,' Maddie said, but a flash of uncertainty in her eyes made my stomach twist up. She squeezed my hand, clearly struggling to find something to say to comfort me. I forced myself to say the next words.

'What if I got it all wrong?'

13

The morning sun had vanished into a grey afternoon twilight and I was freezing. I'd got home goodness knows how much earlier and had been about to hop in the shower when I decided to have the quickest peek at the news.

Hours later, I was shivering in my now pretty manky gym clothes and my eyes were gritting from staring at the screen for so long. I was scouring every last corner of the internet for any mention of Lotta Berglund.

I searched and researched and referenced and cross referenced, following link trails up blind alleyways and scanning more scientific papers than could possibly be good for a person. I deep dove through what appeared to be a cousin's Instagram, screen-grabbing pictures of Lotta Berglund standing stiffly and unsmilingly at the edges of family photos. I skimmed years' worth of Tweets from one of her her colleagues, scrolled through an open Facebook group relating to some scientific conference she had once attended. Pages and pages of my notebook filled with scribbles, notes and arrows, dates circled and places underlined.

Lotta Berglund was a researcher in genetics at the Karolinska Institute, but a deeper dive search had revealed she had a similar degree in bio chemistry as Krister and Mia. I'd have to check with Krister whether he had ever come across her. I sat back, tapping my pen against my teeth as I thought. Science was by no means my thing, but I'd done as much research as I could over the past few months, and thought I had a sort of vague layman's grip on Krister and Mia's world. As far as I could tell, Lotta Berglund had the necessary education to potentially develop the drug used in the murders.

If I was to consider the possibility of being wrong about Mia — just for a moment, just for argument's sake — then the pool of potential killers wasn't huge. The drug narrowed the field significantly. The killer had either come up with or come across a substance unique enough that the police lab technicians had been working for months to identify it with no success. The killer had known what it was, known what it could do, and they had known how to administer it.

When Krister and I had kept vigil together at Johan's bedside after the island, Krister had been restless, unable to sit still or be silent for more than a moment or two. He seemed to get some comfort from focussing on the technical aspects of the murders. He talked for hours, as though addressing an invisible toxicology class, while Johan dozed and I tried desperately to follow information that far exceeded my B in GCSE chemistry.

'It would have to be a drug that breaks down fairly quickly, but not too quickly. The effect must last long enough to kill the victim,' Krister muttered as I stroked Johan's hand and listened to him breathing. 'Breaking down too slowly slowly would complicate the dosage, though that does not matter if the object is to kill a person.' His voice was a low monotone. He frowned, as though flipping through an index in his brain. 'It must be something similar to digitalis.'

'Is Mia familiar with, uhh, that?' I'd asked gently and he looked away.

'It would need to be a large dose to work very quickly, ' he continued as though I hadn't spoken. 'Not all the victims had a post mortem, but those that did came up clear other than any medication they were already taking.

'So either it has a very fast degradation, or it is a substance difficult to find unless you are looking for it.' He'd stroked his chin absentmindedly. I could hear his stubble scratching in the quiet hospital room. 'Something derived from digitoxin, perhaps.' He'd lapsed into silence and we had both watched Johan sleep for a while.

Shivering now, I yanked the duvet from the air mattress and wrapped it around my shoulders. I had a thumping headache from staring at the screen in semi darkness for too long.

I opened up Ola Andersson video Maddie had sent. He was speaking Swedish of course, so I only got the gist of what he was saying. I'd ask Johan or Lena for a translation at some point, but for now, I wasn't interested in the words.

I muted the sound and maximised the screen, staring at his expression as he spoke. At one point he had looked directly at the camera, and I paused it there. He was standing dead on to the camera, his arms by his side, palms facing forward as he spoke in a gesture that struck me instinctively as open. He was of medium height, and with his neat hair and moustache struck me as the type my mum describes as a 'quiet little man.'

'You could do worse than a quiet little man,' she'd once told me as I sobbed my heart out over a break up with an aspiring actor who'd earnestly informed me that to take his career to the next level he needed a girlfriend who was infinitely more fabulous than me. 'They might not set the world on fire, but they'll be kind to you,' she had added with a disapproving sniff.

Was Ola Anderson kind, I wondered, as I unpaused the video and watched him begin to speak again.

I'd read once, that body language tells are complex and subtle and vary from person to person, so the idea that everyone scratches their nose when they are lying, for example, is dubious. On the other hand, the same article suggested that our instincts are generally right. If a person's stance and gestures strike us as truthful, then it's statistically likely to be the case.

I leaned back against my bed as I watched the video and realised that my gut feeling was telling me he was genuine. Ola Andersson believed what he was saying. He believed that Lotta Berglund was the killer.

Not Mia.

I rubbed my temples, not entirely proud of the way my heart leapt at the thought. Mia innocent. Johan would be so thrilled, so relieved. Things might even get back to normal.

Lotta Bergland had a Facebook page, but the only public posts I could see were shares of articles form scientific journals. There was a small handful of photos tagged of her, mostly from professional or family gatherings. In all of those, even when she happened to be positioned in the centre of the group, she was still somehow apart. Her hands were always clasped in front of her, and never once was she making physical contact with anyone on either side of her.

So she isn't the life and soul of the party, I thought, staring at her solemn face. That wasn't exactly hard evidence she is a serial killer.

I noticed that the date on the photo was nearly four years ago. Lotta posted so seldom that I had scrolled back years without realising. I clicked to scroll a little further, and then I saw it.

Six and a half years ago.

Hej då sverige! Goodbye Sweden.

A picture of an American flag.

14

What nobody understands is that I do not chose this. It is incredible that anyone would imagine I would want to live like this, isolated, miserable, alone. This was done to me.

All I want, all I ever wanted, was to be free to do the things that make me happy. I don't understand what's so wrong about that. Everyone else gets to live the life they want to. I see them all the time. Friends laughing over beers at a sidewalk bar, couples holding hands across a table, their heads bent close and intimate, children screaming as they roll around in fresh snow. All those people get to smile and laugh and take pleasure in being alive: why not me?

My mother used to explain that I wasn't different, I was special. 'You're not like other kids, you're better than all of them,' she would whisper, stroking my hair as I fell asleep. 'You'll see. You're going to do great things and then everybody will finally know what you are.'

The problem is that there is no value in being special when the world rewards the unspecial. All those idiots I see every day, laughing and holding hands and screaming in the snow are are the basic, standard issue population. Minimum viable people. Humans level one.

I once had a teacher who didn't grade us in the regular way with A, B or C, but by a system she made up. Excellent. Promising. Ordinary. Fail. The people who populate the world are Ordinary. Most days I can barely tell them apart, and yet they have what I don't. They are rewarded for their dullness.

Sometimes, I let myself imagine the world as it should be. A society ruled by survival of the fittest, in which only the truly deserving obtained money, prestige, a mate. Not those who were born rich and attractive, but those who have original thoughts, who dare to live outside the prescriptions of society.

The mass produced humans wouldn't know what hit them.

All those square-jawed guys and neat little women with their ponytails and gleaming sneakers. Their suburban houses and fluffy children and bouncing dogs would evaporate overnight, and they would be wandering around dazed, heartsick, lonely. Wondering how they could have had everything and it was just taken away for no reason.

Then they would know how I feel, and I would laugh and laugh and laugh.

15

The temperature had risen sharply overnight and the whole world was grey, the city dripping as though it needed a hanky. I sloshed my way through ankle-deep slush, feeling the icy water seep through my boots. I felt as though I'd tramped for miles and my feet were throbbing as well as being freezing and wet. As I stepped into the toasty little café with its inviting smell of coffee and cinnamon, I decided I would stay there for a hot drink regardless.

The initial payment for the book proposal I had submitted to Kate had come through. It wasn't a fortune, but it was enough for Sandra and I to mutually agree that nursery school teaching was not my life's work. The next chunk of money would be dependent on the first draft of the book itself, and I was trying not to focus on the chasm between now and then.

I had spent the morning slogging my way through filthy melting snow around St Eriksplan, peeking into every coffee shop that Ola Andersson regularly checked in to. From what I had been able to tell from his Facebook page, he was some kind of developer. He worked on a freelance basis, coding apps for Stockholm's many digital start-ups, and it seemed to be his habit to hunker down for the day in one of four coffee shops. He always checked in by lunchtime, so my plan was simple. I would do a circuit of them all every morning until I found him.

I was in my fourth coffee shop on the third day. I ordered a hot chocolate with real whipped cream and marshmallows for the sugar hit to end all sugar hits, then I turned around and spotted him. The main area that opened onto the street was bright and lively, filled with a large group of students talking Italian, a group of dads trying to control a swarm of toddlers long enough to chug their coffee, and what seemed to be some kind of brainstorming session punctuated by much laughing and gasping. To the left of the counter, past the toilets, was a little back room that seemed to be designated as an office area.

I could just see a handful of silent freelancers typing industriously, some with noise cancelling earphones on. You had to wonder why someone would come out to a café only to block the world out which they could do at home for free, but each to their own. Ola Andersson was at the back of that room, sitting just under a high window, frowning intently at his laptop.

An impatient voice pierced my thoughts. *'Varsågod.'*

I belatedly realised that the young barista had been trying to hand over my hot chocolate, possibly for quite some time. I took it with a murmured *tack*, and spied someone just leaving the table next to Ola Andersson's.

He didn't show any sign of registering my presence as I sat down and faffed about a bit with my laptop and some notebooks. My laptop is about a thousand years old and waking it up can be like raising the dead with all the whirring and freezing and general panicking it needs to do before it allows me to work. I glanced over at his screen as I spooned up some whipped cream, but it was covered with some coding language that didn't mean a thing to me.

'You need to clear some disk space,' said Ola Andersson and I jumped.

'Sorry,' I muttered, 'a million miles away.'

'Your memory is almost full. That machine is old and shit but it will perform a little better if you delete everything from it. Do you have an external drive?'

'I do, somewhere.' I did. I backed up to it at least once a decade.

Ola Andersson shook his head as my laptop had a minor panic attack at the prospect of connecting to that newfangled internet. Up close, his hair and moustache were every bit as neat as they had been on TV. He was a few years older than me, late thirties, maybe forty. He wore a V-necked jumper over a T shirt and jeans that looked as though they had been ironed. Your standard quiet little man outfit. There was a ski jacket on the back of his chair, the arm printed with the logo of a Swedish ski resort. I frowned. Something about the name of the resort rang a bell, though I couldn't for the life of me think why.

Ola Andersson was slouched against the back of his chair, giving me a slightly sardonic, patronising look as though he knew perfectly well how shit I am at bothering to back up my work. The superior effect was belied by the slight sheen of sweat on the back of his neck, the way his hand trembled a touch as he reached for his coffee. Well, he had just accused his girlfriend of being a serial killer, I thought. That was bound to cause a spot of inner turmoil. His eyes darted around the small room as he drank.

'I suppose you recognise me,' he said bluntly, putting his coffee down.

'I didn't at first,' I lied, pointlessly.

'If you are here to abuse me you might as well just fuck off now. I'm not interested in what feminists think of me.'

'I beg your pardon?'

'Feminism isn't about thinking every woman is perfect,' he snapped.

'No, I don't think so either.'

'Tell that to your friends.'

'What, all the other women? Do you think we have meetings?'

He shrugged and turned back to his work.

'I want to help,' I said.

'You don't want to help me. You just want to prove me wrong.'

'I want to find the killer. If you are right about who it is then I want to help you.'

He looked at me warily. I wondered when he'd last had a full night's sleep.

'I'll be honest with you,' I said, meeting his eye evenly. 'Your accusation alone isn't enough to convince me. But if I'm wrong I want to know. What evidence do you have? Can you link Lotta to any of the victims?'

'Who are you?'

'I'm a journalist. I'm writing a book about the murders and I will share your story, if you tell me all of it. How long have you known Lotta Berglund?'

'Two or three years. But we were only dating a few months.'

'How did you meet?'

'At a dinner party.' He laughed, a sharp bark. 'I was there with my wife.'

'Did you become friends right away?'

He shook his head. 'No, she was just someone we ran in

to occasionally for the first couple of years. Lotta is not somebody who has friends.'

'Why not?'

'It is difficult to describe if you don't know her.'

'Try me.'

'She is not a person one can connect with easily. She does not engage with the world. That first night, at the dinner party, everyone was talking about *Melodifestivalen*. Lotta had never even heard of it.'

Melodifestivalen is the pre Eurovision singing competition that Sweden holds every year to pick their entry. As a country, they are more passionate about The Eurovision Song Contest than is strictly dignified, but their enthusiasm gave us ABBA, so I forgive them.

'Not being interested in *Melodifesivalen* isn't exactly a classic sign of a serial killer,' I pointed out.

'Not being interested, sure, I don't give a fuck about it. But she had never heard of it. She was staring at us all like we were crazy. And that is just one example. She lives in a world inside her head. She does not have emotions like a normal person, she does not care about anyone. The only time I heard her laugh was at my uncle's funeral when the pallbearers tripped and almost dropped the coffin.'

'But you had a relationship?'

'I would not exactly call it a relationship.' There was a little tightness at the corner of his mouth, almost as though he wanted to say more but was trying to trap the words inside.

'So what would you call it?'

'Do you know the term fuck buddies?'

Somehow I kept a straight face. 'I've heard of it.'

He gave a bitter smile. I had a sneaking suspicion that keeping things at fuck buddy level was Lotta's choice. I nodded, disappointment slithering through me. His spite was almost palpable, it danced in the air between us.

'She knows the drug,' he said suddenly. 'If you are researching the case then you know that the killer used a drug that causes an instant heart attack to murder her victims. Lotta switched her focus to genetics a few years ago when she moved home from the US.'

'Where in the US did she live?'

'Boston. She was working on a project at Harvard.'

Excitement prickled over me and it was an effort to keep my expression steady. Maybe I'd been wrong about him. Just because he was spiteful didn't mean he wasn't on to something.

'She quit the project with no warning and abandoned her field altogether,' he continued. 'She had been working on a new heart medicine that she was passionate about. It was rejected because it was deemed too volatile to have therapeutic use, and her team lost their funding. Lotta was furious, convinced that it was all political, that if they could have continued to develop it a little bit more they would have solved heart disease and won a Nobel prize. She was so angry that she stormed out and caught the next plane home to Sweden.'

'I take it you told the police this?'

He nodded. So Henrik would have made the connection with the victim in Boston too. 'The idiot detectives said it was not enough evidence,' he spat, 'but they do not know Lotta like I do.'

He turned to face me fully, his expression hard. 'You have never met anyone as cold as she is,' he said quietly. 'She could kill a person and it would mean so little to her she would forget an hour later.'

16

I was coming home tonight on the T-bana. The carriage was busy and I was forced to stand. I was stuck face to face with a woman, one of the worst kind. An identikit, mass produced human. Dark blond hair scraped back from her face in a pony tail, little to no makeup, no jewellery, sensible winter coat.

She met my eyes as she boarded the train, and she smiled briefly. A habitual twitch of the facial muscles. The most basic gesture of courtesy; the most insulting. I would have been impressed if she had recoiled. Snarled, screamed in horror, laughed in my face. Anything to suggest even a little authenticity. It is a compliment to call these people sheep. Sheep have more individuality than these humans who chose to dress alike and think alike and live alike.

The woman took an e-reader from her bag and got lost in her book as the carriage rocked and swayed its way beneath the city. I watched her read, saw how her pupils raced back and forth, her eyes widening. She bit her bottom lip then glanced up, met my gaze with a guilty flush.

She was reading something dirty, I realised with a heave of disgust. The hand that held her book bore a wedding ring. It was a plain gold band, the kind that is out of fashion now, probably inherited from a parent or grandparent. So she had a husband or a wife at home and yet she felt the need to read filth on her commute home.

I hated her.

Clarity bit at me and I nearly laughed out loud.

I hated her.

Of course I hated her, she was an asshole. It was to be expected. It was a natural reaction. The sheer joy of feeling something, something clear and obvious and real after so long swirled around me like a ribbon and I wanted to kiss her. I wanted to hold her face in my hands and thank her.

Then I realised that what I really wanted to do was kill her.

She got off the train at Slussen to change lines, and I got off too even though it wasn't my stop. As I followed her along platform, I thought about how easy it would be to pretend to stumble and push her into the path of an incoming train. Her scream would be swallowed by the roar of the engine. The driver would slam the brakes on but it would be too late. Her body would be crunched and crumpled under the unrelenting weight of the train. The driver would have nightmares for the rest of his miserable life.

The platform was so crowded at peak commuter time that nobody could ever be certain it was me. I would become one of the crowd. I would scream and cover my mouth and shake my head sadly. I would pretend to care just like the rest of them. I might even hug or rub the back of somebody near me, feel how fragile their bones, how soft and pliable their flesh under the guise of comfort.

But what if they could tell? What if, despite the crowd, someone happened to be looking in my direction when I pushed?

What if they started to yell for the police, to point at me; what if some young, strong idiot took it upon himself to tackle me to the ground and shove my face into the stinking platform?

That was when I got my idea.

17

The next day, I waited across the road from Lotta Berglund's flat. She lived in an olive tenement building in the same style as Johan's, but down at the other end of Södermalm, near Hornstull. Her road was quiet, behind the main road where the shopping centre was, and a church with striking twin steeples rose overhead at the far end. The sun was out again and the fresh snow from the night before was crackling as it melted a microscopic amount, but the air was still bitterly cold. I could feel my nose hairs start to freeze, which was a sensation I hadn't known existed until a few weeks ago and probably could have lived without ever experiencing.

I wasn't entirely sure what I was doing there. Even if I managed to slip into the building, there was no way a woman accused of several murders would just answer her door and invite me in for a chat. I had to start somewhere though, and often, a vague nose about was as good a start as any.

The papers were full of the murders and Ola's accusation. The professional headshot most of the news outlets were using was of Lotta staring evenly into the lens. She was smiling faintly, with a slightly patient air, as thought the photographer had asked her to smile and she found it a ridiculous suggestion, but had decided to indulge him.

I tried to picture Lotta Berglund going about her life in the midst of all of this. Did she just get up and go to work as normal this morning? Had she been swarmed by news cameras and reporters as she bought her morning coffee then headed into the T-bana station? Did she smile that patronising smile, refusing to dignify the babble of questions with so much as acknowledgment? Was she at work now, lost in her research, oblivious to anything but the data on the screen in front of her?

Or had she stayed home? Maybe she was up there, beyond one of those dark windows, shivering under her duvet, streaming mindless soaps from the 90s and eating cereal straight from the box. Would she replay Ola's accusation over and over in her mind, trying to understand how he could do such a thing after what they had? Was she wondering desperately where her life had taken such a horrifying turn, trying and failing to imagine a time when things were normal again?

I thought about what Maddie had said about how the significant other is both the best and worst person to judge guilt, and I wondered how Lotta Berglund had felt when she saw Ola's speech. Had she felt stunned, numb, betrayed, furious? Had she wanted to cry, scream or smash something? Or had she simply nodded, accepting the objective fact of his accusation and knowing that the evidence would disprove it?

A police patrol car pulled up in front of Lotta's building. Two uniformed officers got out and approached the door, their breath visible in the fading afternoon sun. Was this it?

Had they found evidence that implicated Lotta and were here to arrest her?

I shook my head, feeling my neck stiff with the cold. Two young uniformed officers wouldn't be bringing in a suspected serial killer. The street would be crawling with police, radios crackling and lights flashing. Henrik and Nadja would be in charge.

I'd been standing still long enough for the cold to penetrate the gigantic coat my mum gave me for Christmas.

'They're hundreds of pounds normally,' she'd told me gleefully as I unwrapped the bulky package, 'but Lesley and I went to that outlet place where Lesley's daughter got her wedding dress, and got it for practically nothing. They even knocked another tenner off for that wonky zip. You don't even really need a zip on the pocket, do you?'

She'd done her little dance of joy and Johan had watched in bemusement.

I was already living in my little flat by Christmas, but for the week we spent in London it was as though everything evaporated and for a few brief, precious days, we were just us again. Johan had given me a gorgeous pair of vintage earrings for Christmas, and a Swedish phrase book he had annotated to include swear words and dirty jokes.

I watched now as the two police officers emerged from Lotta Berglund's building and headed back to their car with a decidedly unhurried air. This wasn't right. The woman had been accused of up to ten murders. There should be tension. Guns poised. Sweating brows.

When the patrol car crunched off over the packed snow, I slipped across the road. There was a thin coating of frost over the code keypad, so I could see quite clearly which buttons had been pressed lately. After two tries, I got the combination right and was buzzed into Lotta Bergland's building.

The brass-plated list of residents announced Bergland on the fourth floor. It somehow felt too brazen to take the lift when I had no right to be inside the building, so I jogged up the stairs, grudgingly thanking Maddie for dragging me to her fitness hellholes enough that I made it to the fourth floor without bursting a lung. There were four flats on the landing. I could hear high pitched children's voices squealing behind the one to the far left, but the other three were shrouded in silence.

Lotta Berglund's flat was to the far right. A strip of crime scene tape had been placed at a neat diagonal across it, but there was no other sign of activity, no one guarding the door. I crouched down, and briefly crossing my fingers that I wasn't about to come eye to eye with either a serial killer or detective, I pushed up the brass letter box covering and peered inside.

I couldn't see much. The hallway was shadowy, each door leading from it carefully closed. The hardwood floor was covered in a rug I recognised as IKEA, a coat stand in the corner was heaving with the usual assortment of winter coats, hats, scarves, gloves. There was a pile of snow boots and shoes beneath it. Something about their arrangement made me think they had been scattered by the search and put back haphazardly by a careless officer.

There was no sign of life. If her flat had been designated a crime scene, she must have gone to stay with family or friends. I pictured myself knocking on my mum's door with a rueful grin. Just been accused of a few murders. Mind if I stop in my old room a night or two while they search my flat?

I walked back down the stairs slowly, feeling vaguely as

though I were missing something. I was inside Lotta Berglund's apartment building. I didn't want to leave without taking full advantage, but without being able to get inside her flat, what else could I do?

I hovered in the lobby, pretending to read the noticeboard, which was full of the usual fire escape maps and notes from irritated residents imploring neighbours to *please* keep the noise down after 10pm. Just as I was about to give up, I spied an elderly lady heading downstairs with a basket of laundry, and impulsively followed her.

She unlocked the laundry room door and I darted forward to hold it open for her. She gave me a brief smile and I fumbled in my bag for a pen as though I were going to sign up for a laundry time. Swedish apartment buildings all have basement laundry rooms like this, which residents reserve for time blocks of a couple of hours, sometimes weeks in advance. Booking your desired time is a matter of stiff competition, and I have heard of lifelong grudges started by one resident's things being left still in the dryer when their neighbour's *tvättid* had begun.

I ran my finger through the calendar. Lotta Berglund had booked a laundry time two weeks from now. So she hadn't been poised to go on the run.

'*Stackars Lotta,*' murmured the old lady, glancing over my shoulder as she separated her whites. She was heavyset, with long grey hair in a plait wound round her head like a Alpine milkmaid, and wore the kind of flowery housecoat normally found on housewives in sitcoms from the seventies. She tutted and shook her head.

I recognised the phrase, though it took a moment or two for my brain to process it, during which time I'm fairly sure I stared at her with a look of vague terror. Finally I clicked: poor Lotta. I gave a sympathetic sigh.

'This must be awful for her,' I said with a brief smile. 'Sorry, I understand some Swedish but no one seems to understand me if I try to speak.'

The woman waved my apology away as she slammed the washing machine door. 'I was an English teacher for thirty years,' she smiled. 'Then I taught all my grandchildren alongside Swedish so they were bilingual from the beginning. I think it is so important in our world today.'

'I wish I'd learned another language as a small child,' I said. 'I know about seven words of French. It's embarrassing really.'

'It does not matter so much when you already speak English,' she shrugged, filling another machine.

'Have you been in touch with Lotta, since —? I mean, do you know how she is doing?'

The woman frowned. 'Do you know her?'

'No, not really. I've just been following on the news. I can't imagine how awful it must be for her hearing everything they are saying about her.'

'Hopefully she has not heard any of it.'

'Oh, did she — go away somewhere?'

'I hope so.'

'What do you mean?'

Suspicion darted into the woman's eyes. 'What is your name?'

'Ellie James. I am a journalist. I am writing a book about the murders and I would like to interview Lotta if I could, get her side of the story.'

'Well that is impossible. She has been missing since the first night the police came.'

18

'I've got a book deal,' I told Johan.

We were sitting in a rickshaw fashioned into a table at one of my favourite restaurants in Johan's neighbourhood, nibbling our starters of Thai scampi. Though we were on a side street in Stockholm with snow falling outside, inside there was sand on the floor and everywhere was strewn liberally with plastic flower vines and coconut shells. If I squinted, and tried really, really hard, I could almost pretend we were back in Thailand, in those first heady weeks of our relationship where the real world melted into a haze of lust and happiness. I reached over to stroke his cheek.

'Ellie that is amazing.' His face lit up. I searched his eyes but found nothing but happiness. He clinked his beer bottle against mine. 'I am so pleased for you.'

'What if I end up coming to the conclusion that I believe Mia to be the killer?' I said quickly. I'd danced around this subject with him for long enough.

'There is some evidence against Lotta Berglund, but

what if it isn't enough? What if I find something else that incriminates Mia?'

Johan went quiet for a moment, and the hubbub of the restaurant faded as little nerves stabbed along my spine.

'Then you must write what you believe,' he said quietly. 'I trust your skills. You will discover the truth.'

'Do you think the truth is that Mia is innocent?'

He glanced away, suddenly focussing inordinately on dipping the last bit of scampi in chilli sauce. 'Did you read that Lotta Berglund has taken off?' he asked. I nodded.

'She was last seen leaving her apartment minutes after the news broke about her ex's accusation. Disappearing like that is not exactly the actions of an innocent woman, is it? If I were accused of something I would want to be questioned immediately to clear it up.'

'It's easy to say that when you're sitting here not accused of anything,' I pointed out. 'I'd like to think I would too, but people don't always do the sensible thing when they're scared. An old police contact of mine in London once told me that it's the person who behaves impeccably in an interrogation he has his eye on. The ones that are willing to answer anything and remember every detail perfectly are more likely to have planned their answers. Normal people get flustered. If you're not expecting to be interviewed by the police, you forget stuff, get mixed up, or get angry or defensive for all sorts of reasons that don't mean you're guilty of a crime.'

'Okay,' he nodded, took a slug of his beer, 'so I could accept she panicked and ran the first night. But it has been two days now. She would have come to her senses and contacted a friend or family member by now.'

I refrained from reminding him that Mia had been missing for over five months.

We broke off as our main courses were delivered. I took my first bite and my mouth was instantly set on fire. I croaked pathetically and Johan chuckled and handed me my beer. He'd warned me against ordering a dish with three chillis next to it and I'd airily told him the spicier the better. He sensibly resisted reminding me of this.

'The very first time I came here, I ordered a dish with three chillis on the menu,' he said as I gulped my beer and felt sweat break out along my hairline. 'It was almost twenty years ago. There was a big group of us from school, celebrating the end of exams or someone's birthday, I don't remember. All the boys were daring each other to order the hottest dish. Of course I accepted the challenge, then I ate maybe five mouthfuls with tears streaming down my face, sweat everywhere, just doing all I could not to start crying for my mother.' I giggled at his pained expression. 'This one guy whose name I can't even think of now, but he was the star of the football team —'

'The most popular guy in school?' I asked, fluttering my eyelashes.

'Yes, exactly,' Johan rolled his eyes. 'He bet me five hundred crowns that I could not finish the entire meal. I couldn't even speak I was in so much pain, so I just nodded. Of course he shouted for everyone to watch and I honestly believed that I was about to die.

'Then Mia ordered a glass of milk and pretended to knock it over so it went all over my plate. I didn't even know that milk calms the effect of chillies until I started eating again, and none of the guys watching knew either, so I won the five hundred crowns.'

The lights in the restaurant went out, plunging us into blackness for an instant, then flashed like lightning, followed by a sound effect of thunder. It was was a mad effect they did every hour or so, and it was always followed by a rumble of chuckles throughout the restaurant as people laughed at themselves for getting a fright. When the lights came properly back on, I just glimpsed the sadness in Johan's expression before he forced himself to smile again.

'What did you spend your winnings on?' I asked.

'Albums,' he grinned. 'There is a record shop just around the corner that is open late at night. Krister and I went there and I bought *Showbiz* by Muse, Foo Fighters *There is Nothing Left to Lose*, Travis *The Man Who*... and one more.' He scrunched up his nose as he thought. 'Oh yes. *Play* by Moby.'

'How very trendy,' I grinned. I was toying with my meal, trying to nibble at the bits not drenched in the sauce of fire. 'It was nice of Mia to help you out.'

'Nice for a serial killer'

There was a steely edge to his voice that made my stomach twist a little.

'People are complicated,' I said. 'Even serial killers, I reckon. Whatever we eventually find out, it won't make your memories of your friendship and times you spent with her not true any more. They still happened.'

Johan nodded. There was that little tightness to his jaw that always tugged at his guts. He took a bite and chewed with inordinate concentration. 'I'm worried about Krister,' he said. 'I have been for a while. He seems to be getting worse, not better. To begin with he was sad and shocked and hurt, but now he seems so empty. It's like his body still walks and talks but he is not present. I feel as though if he retreats into himself much more he might not come back.'

Worry was etched in the little fine lines around his eyes. I reached over to squeeze his hand. Krister had to be okay, I thought. For Johan's sake if not his own.

'I think it's probably natural for it to get worse before it gets better,' I said, and Johan nodded though he still didn't quite meet my eyes. 'Emotional stuff is rarely linear. I bet that when he seemed to be handling it well, it just hadn't sunk in yet. It's so much to get his head around.

'Johan, I don't believe that we are going to discover she is completely innocent. I am beginning to accept that there is more to the story, but I heard her that day, I saw her hit you. I suspect deep down Krister knows it too.

'But he'll still be feeling confusion over it all, reassessing everything he thought he knew about her. Guilt, probably, that he didn't know. Plus he has to grieve her. It's just like your memories of your friendship with her, maybe the woman he was in love with didn't really exist, but that doesn't mean the love wasn't real to him.'

'You are very wise,' Johan said with a brief smile.

'I am. It's known throughout the land. Did something happen? Is there anything in particular that's made you worried?' I asked.

I'm sure I imagined him hesitating before he shook his head.

19

It is perfect, my plan. It is like a piece of flawless machinery, impeccably designed to achieve precisely what it is meant to in a seamless flow. I can feel it inside me, fizzing and radiant with possibilities.

I went to a watch factory once, on holiday in Switzerland as a child. There was a display which magnified the inner machinery of a fine watch to show how immaculately complex it was. The man behind the display noticed my interest and spoke to me. I couldn't understand all he said; I could already read entire books in English but I was not familiar with his accent.

I grasped, however, how this watch would never need to be wound or have batteries replaced because the workings were so exquisite they would last for infinity. It was the most beautiful thing I had ever experienced. The perfection of it all.

My plan contains some of the same wonder. The perfection is mitigated by the risk involved. That is inevitable. The machinery of my plan consists of people and people always bring the potential for mess and unexpectedness.

But even the possibility of defeat means nothing to me because I have nothing left to lose. I am a husk, a broken shell, *discarded and empty. If nothing has any meaning, then defeat has no meaning.*

I stare out over the sea. It's a little windy today, the waves dance a deep, dark grey under the low sky. I don't know how long I have been sitting here, though the numbness in my body suggests it has been some time.

I am not cold, though. I am never cold any more. The glow of what is to come warms me from within.

Because it is to come. There was no decision to make. As soon as the thought came it was inevitable.

Now it is only a matter of time.

20

I woke with a start and lay for a moment, completely disorientated, trying to figure out what had woken me. I was in that foggy state of a deep sleep disturbed. The silence and stillness suggested was the dead of night.

I blinked a few times as my eyes adjusted and the murky outlines of my weird empty little flat came into focus. My nose and ears were numb with cold, and a thick iciness had penetrated right through me, despite my heavy duvet. I sat up in confusion, fumbling for the bedside lamp as my teeth chattered.

Had the heating gone off? The heating in the apartment building was communal, included in the monthly fee I paid to the residents association. If it had gone off I didn't even know how to go about getting it back on. There must be some kind of emergency contact, but I didn't have the first clue of how to find out.

I reached over and grabbed a fleece jumper I'd conveniently dropped on the floor once upon a time, shivering so much I could hardly catch my breath. I remembered the documentary I'd once watched with my mum about an early

South Pole expedition. One of the last photographs taken of the men showed them huddled together in a tent, icicles on their beards and eyebrows. I knew how they felt, I thought grimly, as I shuddered again, wondering what I should do about contacting the residents association at this time —

Then I saw it.

The blind shifted, just a tiny bit, as a breeze fluttered through the room.

The window was open.

It wasn't possible.

I jumped as the wind blew again with more force, and a gust of snow scattered over the windowsill. I stared, frozen with horror, my heart pounding as though it might burst out my ribcage.

My breath caught in my chest as I waited, half imagining a shadowy figure about to climb into my room, brandishing a syringe that would catch the light from the street lamps outside before —

Oh for heaven's sake, I told myself crossly. The flat was on the third bloody floor. Anyone about to come through that window would have to be Spiderman. There wasn't even a balcony below the window.

I shuddered as the unwelcome image popped into my head of a creature crouching at the edge of next door's balcony, its arms snaking two, three metres along the wall to catch hold of my bedroom window.

The window had been locked tight all winter. I'd moved in to the flat in late November when it was already much too chilly to consider letting fresh air in. It was a modern window, double glazed. Even if someone had somehow reached it from the outside they wouldn't have been able to open it.

Unless they opened it from the inside.

Propelled by sheer terror I scrabbled from the air mattress, stumbling in my terror and smashing my knee against the hardwood floor. I slammed the window shut and pulled the lock tight. The room was still bitterly cold. I shivered in my pyjamas even with the fleece jumper on as I froze, listening intently for any noise, any movement.

There was something.

Chills of pure fear rippled through me as I strained my ears, wondering what in the hell I was going to do if it turned out to be —

Someone snoring. My upstairs neighbour, whose snores reverberated around the building most nights. I rolled my eyes at myself, nearly laughed with relief as I heard him snort and fart as he rolled over.

After our Thai dinner that evening, I'd gone back to Johan's and we had shared a bottle of wine as he poured out stories. We'd sat at the kitchen table and I held his hand in mine as he talked and talked and I felt closer to him than I had in a long time. The wild Midsummer Krister was arrested after hitching a lift on the back of a rubbish truck, naked. The time he and Liv argued over whose turn it was to mop the floor and she ended up dumping the bucket of dirty water on his head. The weekend Mia finally agreed to move in with Krister but refused to hire a moving van because it was just a few blocks, so they had trekked back and forth for hours carrying a box each at a time. Sometime on the Sunday afternoon, it had been discovered that a bottle of olive oil had broken and had been dripping all they way, so there was what appeared to be a permanent trail staining the pavement between the two apartments.

'Well at least I will always find my way home if you annoy me,' Mia had laughed.

I hadn't stayed over though. It had been in the air, the

possibility, but I'd had this gut feeling that he needed to be alone with his memories, so I left. When I got back to the flat I'd sat by the window a few minutes, staring out at the darkness, wondering if I'd done the right thing, or if I should get dressed again and go scampering over the snow to get to him.

I must have opened the window then. I couldn't remember doing so, but it was the obvious explanation. Between the beers at dinner and the wine after I'd been a bit foggy. I must opened the window then not shut it properly afterwards and sometime when I was asleep the wind had blown it open again.

I'd nearly frozen myself to death because I was a drunken idiot who'd decided not to sleep with her boyfriend, I thought, rolling my eyes. Only I could risk bloody hypothermia inside my own bed. Now that the window was closed, the temperature had risen a few degrees, but it would be a while before it was comfortable enough to sleep.

I yanked on my trusty giraffe onesie and some thick ski socks and made myself a cup of tea, then curled under the covers, feeling my insides slowly thaw out as I sipped. I'd left the blinds open, and when I turned the lamp off a smattering of stars pierced the dark purple sky.

You never saw stars that bright in London, I thought, and a wave of homesickness washed over me. I felt a sudden yearning for light pollution and filthy streets and comforting telly and supermarkets that made sense and people who asked strangers if they were alright. A world where I had half a dozen people to text when I needed a partner in crime for a cheeky after work wine on any given evening. Where I didn't know any serial killers and I slung men out the minute they'd caught their breath. Life was so much simpler when I waved them off with a cheery *lovely to have met you, thanks for all the shagging. Bye now, don't forget your pants. Tube station's that way.*

I heaved a miserable sigh and watched my breath cloud the icy air. What on earth was I doing in this strange, freezing, dark country with its rules I still hadn't fully grasped almost a year on, its murderers and its Johans? I loved him with a force that took my breath away, but I didn't know how to be with him through this. It was too big, too bizarre, too much. I always got it wrong. I gave him space when he needed me, crowded him when he couldn't take it.

My tea had gone cold but the rest of me was almost defrosted. I was wide awake though, so I reached for my laptop and waited the inevitable age for it to clank to life. It crossed my mind I should probably have taken Ola Andersson's advice and cleared some memory, and my lip curled as I remembered his patronising smile.

Then I remembered his ski jacket, and something pinged in my brain.

I opened up my Notes app, where I had made a list of all the victims.

Karin Söderström, 15. Exposure following asthma attack. Sälen.

Sven Olafsson, 49. Died of an asthma attack in Tantolunden Park

Annette Björkstedt, 38. Fell down the stairs opposite Fotografiska, catastrophic head injury.

Cattis Bergman, 23. Complications from an epileptic seizure at home on Skånegatan.

Sigge Åstrand, 34. Heart attack at Kvarnen.

Björne Svensson, 29. Overdose at home on Åsögatan

Sanna Johansson, 30. Drowned following heart failure in straight near Arholma.

Gustav Lindström 30. Instant heart failure at Nytorget.
Liv Nilsson, 31. Instant heart failure at home on Hornsgatan.
I added two more names:
Anna Essen, 23. Cause of death unknown. Found posed at Mariatorget.
Mattius Eklund, 20. Cause of death unknown. Found on a bench in front of Stora Blektornsparken.

Karin Söderström was the victim the most damning for Mia. She had been in the same class as Mia, Johan, Krister and Liv. She'd had a crush on Johan, and he had told me he had been sort of interested too, in that awkward teenage boy way which had consisted mostly of him ignoring her and occasionally making fun of her. During the school ski trip, Krister had conspired to shove the two of them onto a ski lift together, and they had stammered and stuttered their way towards a plan to meet late that evening for a walk. When evening came Johan chickened out and Karin had been found dead the next morning on the cross country ski trail where they had agreed to meet.

I had managed to find potential links between Mia and a few of the other victims, but given that they all lived on one small island where people's lives inevitably crisscrossed, I knew that few, if any, would hold up in court. Karin Söderström, however, had been killed on the outskirts of a remote mountain village. Mia had been there; it was unlikely Lotta Berglund had been.

But Ola Andersson owned a ski jacket bearing the name of the same resort.

21

'It's not one of the well known resorts,' I explained to Henrik and Nadja the following evening at the police station. We were in the same little interview room where they had questioned me after Gustav Lindström's death, and I was almost certain that the manky coffee Henrik had handed me was the same one from back then too.

'It's near Salén, but it's off the beaten track. This afternoon I spoke to Josefin Beckman, the principal at their school who was on the trip, and she explained that one of the teachers had a family connection to this little village, so they got a good deal.'

'And this jacket Ola Andersson wears, is it only available at the resort itself?' Nadja asked. Henrik was taking notes.

I nodded. 'It's part of the uniform that the ski instructors wore. Josefin Beckman put me in touch with the owners, and it turns out they don't have a ski school there any more, but bus guests to one of the bigger resorts. They only ever had four or five instructors, so the owner remembers Ola well. He was working there over the season when Karin Söderström died. The owner couldn't remember offhand whether or not Ola was working the week of the school trip, but he said he would try to dig out the rota from that period to confirm. I told him you would probably follow up.'

'That was kind of you,' said Nadja tartly.

'Thank you for bringing this to us now,' added Henrik, with a mild warning look at Nadja. He sat back in his chair which creaked under his weight and stretched. I noticed that his shirt was crumpled, and he had several days' worth of salt and pepper stubble.

'I researched an article about serial killers a few years ago,' I continued. 'It was some anniversary to do with the Yorkshire Ripper, I wrote a piece about some of the more famous ones, trying to explore just why they fascinate us so much. In my research, I came across the fact that because of their narcissism, it is very common for them to be fascinated by what they have done. Very often they will insert themselves into the investigation somehow, in the guise of a helpful witness. Ted Bundy did that. The public way that Ola accused Lotta Berglund — he didn't just come to you quietly, he called a press conference — there was something odd about it.'

'He does not have the education in chemistry to have developed the drug,' said Nadja.

'True, but he knew Lotta, who did. What if she unwittingly helped him and threatened to turn him in when she realised? What if that's why she has disappeared?'

The two detectives exchanged a look.

'Has there been any sign of her yet?'

'Her debit card was used at a cash machine in the Netherlands yesterday,' Nadja said shortly. 'There was no indication of an altercation at her apartment. Our belief at the current time is that she left of her own accord, perhaps hoping that the attention from his accusation would die down.'

'We have spoken to many of her colleagues, family members, who say it is not uncommon for her to take off for a trip without telling anyone,' Henrik added.

'There's more,' I said. 'Ola got the job as the ski instructor because his uncle was friends with the owner. This uncle is a funeral director in a small town just outside Gothenburg, and Ola had worked for him the summer before.'

'In the funeral parlour?'

I nodded. 'He told me that a trainee like Ola was not qualified to embalm of course, but that he would have been present, even assisting, many times. He could well have picked up the basics.'

'We have checked Ola Andersson's passport records and he was not in the US when the victim in Boston was killed,' said Henrik.

'I've been thinking about that — what if that's a red herring? What if these two murders aren't linked to that one, but copycats? Lotta was there, she must have read or heard about it. She could have told him about it and that's where he got the idea from. He made a point of telling me that she was in Boston at the time.'

'You have spoken to him?' Nadja looked up sharply, her eyes narrowed.

'I ran into him at a coffee shop,' I said, with a slightly defensive shrug. 'We're both freelancers. We fell into conversation.'

I would have judged them if they'd believed that. Nadja shot an irritated glance at Henrik and seemed just about to lay into me when his phone buzzed. He glanced at it and his eyes widened.

'We have to go,' he said, getting to his feet. He snapped

something in rapid Swedish at Nadja. I caught '*kropp*' and '*Skanstull*.'

Another body had been found at Skanstull.

As soon as their patrol car pulled away from the police station, I started jogging in the direction of Skanstull.

THE OUTDOOR SWIMMING pool was covered up for the winter, the large fenced off area flat with thick snow. I'd guessed that if a body had been posed near Skanstull it would have to be in the area between Ringvägen and the water, a little way back from the heavily trafficked junction. Hoping to avoid Henrik or Nadja spotting me, I'd run down to the water at the other side of the bridge, then jogged back under the cycle path, passing the boat club with its rows of silent boats trapped in ice, and the outdoor gym. In the summer it was buzzing round here with sunbathers and joggers and swimmers, but now the silence was almost palpable.

The main sidewalk that ran between the leisure centre and the outdoor pool was guarded by uniformed officers, but I clambered up a treacherously icy pathway at the other side, past the little red allotment cottages that peeked out from beneath pristine snow. I finally got high enough to be able to see the crime scene flooded with silver light and paused, breathing heavily, sweating in my thick coat as I watched the now horribly familiar hive of activity.

A group of Scene of Crime officers carried a white tent across the open space, but just before they unfurled it, I caught a glimpse of the victim. The woman — I was almost positive it was a woman, though at such a distance it was difficult to be certain — was upright like the others, but she lurched heavily to one side. Was she in some kind of leaning pose — dancing? Yoga? — or had she simply fallen over?

The tent went up and I swore under my breath as she was hidden from view. I was almost sure she had fallen. Not fallen, in fact. Collapsed. Her neck was horribly bent as though her head was too heavy to support; one arm had been pointed high, but the other just flopped at her side, as though she were a puppet whose strings had broken.

The other two had been so flawlessly posed. The killer was slipping. Had they rushed this time, failed to dose the body with quite enough freezing chemical to achieve the full statue effect?

My thighs were burning from crouching in the snow, so I stood up, hoping that I was far enough away to escape attention. There probably wasn't much else I could see now that the tent was up, I thought, realising that feeling in my toes had departed several minutes earlier. I should go, write up my notes on this latest development. I'd passed on what I knew to the police, it was up to them to take action on it.

Then I heard a noise and I froze, icy chills trickling down my spine.

I wasn't alone up here.

A footstep, crunching through snow, just behind me. This path was too steep to be heavily used in the winter, the snow had been undisturbed when I'd scrabbled my way up. Behind me was only allotments, the nearest apartment buildings a good twenty, thirty metres away.

I turned slowly, my heart hammering, and I came face to face with Ola Andersson.

22

'How strange to meet you again here,' he said in an unnaturally bright tone. He stood a foot or two away, his hands stuffed into the pockets of his ski jacket.

Spiders of terror scuttled down my spine as I desperately attempted to arrange my features into some sort of smile. He turned and stared at the silvery glow of the crime scene in the distance with a slight frown, as though he had just noticed it.

'I wonder what is happening over there?' he asked.

'I — don't know,' I muttered. I forced a grin that I'm certain seemed manic. 'I was just walking by. Got a bit lost. I was going to the, uhh, subway station at Skanstull.' I laughed, my voice shrill. 'Must have taken a wrong turn somewhere.' I was babbling. The words tumbled pointlessly out.

'And you found yourself here,' he said, cocking his head to one side like a curious dog. 'You are very nosy, aren't you Ellie?'

'I'm just lost. I'd better get home, my boyfriend will be wondering where I am. Nice to see you.'

Ola sniggered, but as I made to step past him, he shifted just slightly so that he was in my way. He hadn't torn his eyes from the crime scene for a second. My heart tumbled into my toes.

Out of the corner of my eye I could see Henrik and Nadja striding along the little path that had been trampled in the snow towards the tent where the body was. Look up, I begged silently, even though they'd never see us in the darkness. Ola was standing a little above me on the narrow path. To get towards Ringvägen I would have to push past him. Behind me was only a snow covered beach then the solid ice of Lake Mälaren.

'What do you think happened there?' he asked again, nodding towards the crime scene.

I could run round the way I came, I thought frantically. If I was fast enough, I might just manage to scream to one of the uniformed officers before —

My breath caught in my throat as I imagined an icy syringe being plunged into my neck, the sensation so acute I could almost feel the chill of the chemical invading my body, turning me into a living statue.

And then a dead statue.

'I think someone was murdered,' I said, amazed at how steady my voice sounded.

'That is very sad,' he said in the sort of bright, sing-song voice that reminded me of myself begging little Tor-Björn to stop crying.

'Yes.'

'I suppose it was Lotta who killed her.' He tutted, shaking his head. 'She is very evil. They really should stop her.'

'How do you know it was a woman who died?' I asked quietly. 'They put the tent up before you got here.'

He chuckled, but there was an edge in his voice that sent

chills cascading through me. I could feel terror building in me as though it were a physical thing, suffocating me from the inside. *Don't fucking faint, Ellie*, I ordered myself. This was not the time.

'Do you not know the statistics?' he asked, shaking his head with a soft tut. 'It is always women who die.'

The moon came out from behind a cloud. Our eyes met for the first time and I saw fear trickle into his. We both froze for a split second then he span around and ran up the path.

'Henrik —! Nadja —' I screamed. 'Up here!'

I didn't wait to see if anyone had heard as I gave chase.

There must have been steps cut into the snow. I slipped and jammed my kneecap into solid ice, scrabbled to my feet, skidded and slithered through thick snow as Ola's dark form disappeared into the murk ahead of me. The path widened out at the top of the hill and I saw him pick up the pace.

My lungs were burning already, legs trembling as I sprinted to try to close the gap between us —

He turned suddenly and I screamed — he flung something at me and the sharp shock of pain was dizzying as my cheek was sliced by a jagged icicle —

I could feel hot blood trickling along my jawline, down my neck and the world span and wavered in my vision as I gritted my teeth, forced myself to my feet again —

We crossed the open space and Ola slipped around an apartment building and onto a quiet residential road —

There was a dog walker up ahead who barely glanced up as Ola ran past her.

'Help,' I screeched. 'Call the police!'

But the woman shrank back, dragged her little dog towards the apartment building. Ola was almost at the end of the road.

I could feel a howl of pain and terror and frustration building as I staggered on — the distance between us was growing, Ola appeared to be gaining strength the further he got from me —

He dashed around the corner and burst onto Ringvägen which was bumper-to-bumper with traffic in both directions. He ran into the road, weaving between cars as I gritted my teeth in a final burst of speed —

The number three bus came trundling up the bus lane just as Ola darted from the other side —

The dull thud reverberated through me as Ola's body flew into the air —

A flurry of screams, the screech of brakes —

My legs gave way and I crumpled onto my knees in the snow piled by the side of the road. My blood roared and my own rasping, horrified gasps filled my ears. It seemed as though everything went into slow motion as Ola landed on a jagged pile of snow in front of the bus with a curiously echoing silence and lay completely still.

23

It was morning before I was released. I left the hospital, the stitches in my cheek stinging despite the copious painkillers I had been given in the night. I was drunk with exhaustion, the murky, greyish-purple dawn swimming in my vision. Henrik had said something about a patrol car driving me home earlier, but there was no sign of him when the nurse said I could go, and I couldn't bear to stay in the hospital another moment.

I started to walk home. Ringvägen was still cordoned off and I didn't think I could bring myself to get on a number three bus. As I waited for the green crossing signal, I turned and glanced back at the hospital.

Ola Andersson was somewhere in there, in a coma and under arrest. Henrik had told me that Ola had broken his pelvis, femur and several ribs, one of which had punctured a lung. He was alive though, I thought sourly, which was more than could be said for that poor woman he had left crumpled on top of a closed swimming pool. His ex wife, Ulrika Andersson.

I felt a deep shudder wrack through me and held on to

the traffic light for support. I'd tried to dose on the stretcher while I was waiting for my stitches, but every time I closed my eyes I saw Ola's body fly into the air, heard the screech of the brakes, screams, sirens, Henrik's shout from behind me. Snow dyed dark read with blood.

The pedestrian crossing turned green and I crossed Ringvägen, looking steadfastly ahead so that I didn't so much as glimpse the accident scene. I wasn't familiar with the back roads round here, but vaguely trusted that if I zigzagged generally right I would eventually reach Götgatan and then I'd know where I was again.

'You followed us?' Nadja spat in the emergency room as I lay on a stretcher with gauze pressed to my cheek. Henrik gave her a warning look to keep her voice down, which she silenced with a glare that could freeze lava. 'To an active crime scene? What were you thinking?'

'I just wanted to see,' I'd sighed. I couldn't defend myself. Partly because I had already been given some spectacular pain killers and was woozy as hell, but mostly because she was right. 'I stayed far back. I wasn't in the way.'

Somewhere beyond my cubicle an agitated old man argued with medical staff, a baby cried, a monitor beeped urgently. My cheek stung like a bastard and I kept feeling little jerks, like mini electric shocks, as adrenaline drained from my body. Henrik had offered to phone Johan, but I'd refused.

'We could arrest you for obstructing an investigation.'

'I didn't obstruct it. I was just watching. He approached me.'

'You chased him.'

'I screamed for you first. Was I supposed to just stand there and wave him off?'

'What would you have done if you had caught him,

Ellie?' Henrik had asked gently. I'd turned away. I didn't have an answer to that. 'That is why you cannot —'

'I don't know, sat on him until you came?' I spat. My body was trembling and for a horrible moment I thought I was going to cry. 'I didn't really think about it. He ran and I chased. It was instinctive. Anyone would have done this same thing. I should have —'

I cut myself off, bit back the sob I could feel building.

'Should have what?' Henrik asked gently.

'Mia was right there and I let her escape.'

I half caught them exchanging a glance out of the corner of my eye.

'The cottage was on fire and Johan was trapped inside,' Henrik said after a moment. 'I think you made the right choice to help him.'

'It was probably me who knocked the candle over when I ran after her,' I said bitterly. 'I should have tackled her the moment she entered the cottage. I could have locked her in one of the bedrooms or something, I don't know. She was only a couple of metres away from me and I let her get away.'

'We also let her get away.' Henrik perched at the foot of my stretcher as I stared at the ceiling, blinking away tears.

'Yes, you're bloody useless as well.'

'If you had not been there tonight, Ola may have escaped,' Nadja said grudgingly. 'One of our colleagues has informed us that he had three flights booked for this evening. He may well have already left the country before we tried to arrest him.' She met my eye with a brief smile of apology, before her usual stern expression returned.

'He must have already killed his ex when I spoke to him at the coffee shop the other day,' I said with a shudder. 'He was a bag of nerves. He mentioned her. They were still together when he first met Lotta Berglund.'

Ola Andersson had confessed, lying in filthy snow in front of the bus, while an ambulance inched through the gridlocked traffic towards him. He blamed Lotta for supposedly luring him from a marriage he claimed had been happy until he met her, only to dump him weeks later. He had convinced himself that Lotta must then be evil, possessed of some preternatural power over him. When he discovered that Ulrika had met someone new, he realised that he could kill two birds with one stone by killing her and making it seem as though she were one of the serial killer's victims.

'Does he genuinely believe Lotta killed Anna Essen and Mattius Eklund?' I asked.

Nadja nodded. 'So he says. The state of Ulrika's body strongly suggests that she was not murdered by the same killer as the first two. There are indications of a first time killer.'

Ola had injected his ex with insulin stolen from a diabetic colleague. Despite having worked in a funeral home, he hadn't thought of embalming her, had relied instead on rigor mortis. He had killed Ulrika almost two days before posing her, had hid her in his grandmother's allotment cottage next to the swimming pool while he worked up the courage to pose her, so her body had collapsed as rigor mortis began to pass.

'If he has taken Lotta Berglund somewhere, he did not admit it,' Henrik added. 'He swore that he was as surprised as anyone when she disappeared.'

'Couldn't he be lying?'

'It is rare for people to lie when they think they are

dying,' Nadja shrugged, her expression still stern, though worry tugged at her eyes. 'But —'

'He's an unusual guy,' I supplied.

I'd now completely lost my bearings and was climbing a hill which had a small church at the top. The pavement was steep and covered in fresh snow, and I could feel sweat freezing on the back of my neck. It was almost light, and the low mid-morning sun pierced between the buildings, glinting off the church's steeple and making the snow twinkle.

There were people around, heading for work, checking phones, steaming travel mugs of coffee on the other hand, dragging solemn toddlers to nursery on sledges. Up ahead I saw two friends greet each other with warm hugs and laughter that rang through the air. I felt completely removed from it all, as I though I were invisible, able to see the outside world but trapped in a different dimension full of murder and hidden girlfriends and pelvises shattered by buses.

What felt like hours later, I finally spied Nytorget up ahead and knew I was just a few blocks from home. The sun was high in the sky, and the trees lining the walkway I was tramping along were dripping icy water on me, but I didn't have the energy to care. When I reached the square, I decided to nip into the fancy deli, feeling suddenly that some kind of breakfast pastry that involved chocolate was crucial to my immediate survival.

As I passed, I noticed a crowd of people gathered in the square itself, standing more or less where the fountain was in summer. I remembered Johan's mournful look when they covered it up sometime in October, and I'd laughed at him. 'It's just winter.' I'd rolled my eyes. 'It comes every year, and then it will pass.' How young I had been then.

There was an elderly lady standing at the head of the group, addressing them. She was statuesque, with almost military-straight posture, long, pure white hair flowing down her back over her full length winter coat. A tour group, I wondered idly. There was something a little bit intense about her manner to merely be filling them in on the history of the neighbourhood, but perhaps she just took her job very seriously.

As I approached the deli and the smell from the bakery made my knees wobble, a young guy, skinny and sort of angular with a mournful face exaggerated by long, poker-straight dirty blond hair stepped in my path. He held out a flyer with an oddly grave expression. I just glimpsed a photo of the white-haired lady on it as I made to go around him with a sigh of irritation and a muttered '*nej tack*'.

'Do you like living in fear?' he asked in coldly precise English.

'What?'

'Don't you want to not be afraid any more?'

He shoved the flyer in my face and I only just resisted punching him in his.

'I'm fine, thanks,' I snapped and shoved open the door of the deli.

24

The city was filled with anger. She could feel it, fizzing and spitting like acid. It was everywhere, corroding the facade of civility and understanding and fairness. People were afraid and their fear was dragging them inexorably back to their true selves, warriors, hunters, fuelled by vengeance and violence.

It was thrilling.

She felt more alive than she could remember every feeling before. Every cell in her body glowed and vibrated with energy and light. Her eyes shone, her blood rushed, her body thrummed with fire and vitality.

It was what she had been waiting for.

For so many years, the teachers and the doctors and the social workers had tried to get her to be more like other people. It turned out, that what needed to happen was for the other people to become more like her. And now they finally were.

All it took was for a few people to die, she marvelled. Random people, chosen with no rhyme or reason, to lose their lives, and the world began to change. It was the randomness that frightened them, she thought with satisfaction. When there was a pattern, when a misogynist killer targeted sex workers or a right wing fanatic took their inadequateness out on immigrants, it didn't disturb order. People tutted, they sympathised, they lectured colleagues over the morning coffee break about how the justice system had failed society, but they didn't truly care. The victim criteria did not apply to them. It was a terrible story to watch on the news, but not one that truly affected them.

But not now. Now, no one knew who might be next. It could be that smug latte pappa with his baby in an organic hemp sling, the overweight woman pounding the pavements on her morning run. It could be a woman, a man, someone old or young. Maybe even a child.

The thought stopped her short. A child. The death of a child would really set a cat amongst the pigeons.

Even she would probably be troubled by the death of a child.

The only person she had ever felt anything for was the little girl. It had been the strangest sensation, to look at this podgy, partly-formed human and — what was it, exactly? Had she recognised something in her? Some connection between them. Or was it simply that the little girl was the only person not to look at her with fear and suspicion? As soon as the door was opened, she would hear the little girl's footsteps scampering over the floor as she ran with delighted squeals into her arms, and she would feel — something.

The teachers and the doctors and the social workers had all believed that she hated Lisbet and Mamma and Pappa, but she didn't. She felt nothing for them. Just an empty hole. Pappa had always been nice to her, so she had tried to make herself cry at his funeral, but nothing came. Eventually she had settled on a sort of low wailing which she found she enjoyed. She'd got really rather into it, keening and moaning, letting her voice go high and low, liking the feel of the ticklish vibrations in her throat. She had barely noticed the looks being exchanged on the other pews.

But she hadn't cared that he was dead. She hadn't known how. Nobody ever taught her.

The little girl, however, she would care very much if the little girl died. She wasn't sure she would miss her, exactly, she didn't see her very much any more after all, but she was almost certain that if the little girl became an ice statue in the snow it would upset her terribly. Just thinking about it made her want to wail like she had at Pappa's funeral, but she couldn't risk people noticing her right now.

She had got so much better at blending in to crowds. Sometimes, she was so good at it that she wondered if she had become invisible. Then someone would hold a door or glance in her direction and she knew that they could see her. It was just that they couldn't see what she truly was.

25

My lungs were fit to burst and my cheek throbbed like it was on fire, but I kept running. I'd got home finally and collapsed so hard on the air mattress that it had skidded about a foot across the hardwood floor. I'd lain staring at the sun-dappled ceiling for goodness knows how long before I'd given up and headed out.

I was too tired to sleep. Drained but buzzing. I wanted to sleep forever but I was afraid of what I'd see when I closed my eyes.

I just needed to exhaust myself a bit more, I'd decided. A bit of bracing fresh air would send me over and then when I woke up I would be able to think straight again.

I'd kept to busy roads, pounding pavements so well-trodden that the tarmac showed through gritty ice. I'd headed up Folkungagatan, where traffic inched and pedestrians swarmed in and out of the T-bana station. I'd done a loop around Medborgarplatsen. I'd passed Johan's old school, then headed down a little side street to avoid Maria-torget, emerging on to Hornsgatan and nearly colliding with a gaggle of bikes waiting at the traffic light to cross Slussen.

It was about then I finally admitted I was dizzy and one of my calf muscles had seized up, so I slowed to a walk to cross Slussen and climb Katrinavägen. I paused at the top of the hill to look over the cliff at the city laid out below me. The harbour shimmered in the sun and the cramped little buildings of the old town looked like the cover of a box of chocolates, their bright colours peeking out from beneath a blanket of snow.

'It's always the most obvious solution,' Archie MacLean, my old pal at the Met police in London had told me once. He'd been a detective since the year dot, and when I knew him he was cheerfully old and bitter, spending more time in the pubs around Fleet Street bitching about the state of the force than he did solving any crimes. He was a giant of a man, with a bulbous nose covered with broken capillaries, who'd park himself at the bar and wait for the inevitable stream of crime reporters who would buy him Islay malts all day long in exchange for his insights on whatever story they were working on. A grumpy old lush of an investigative genius, he tripped and drowned in the Thames on the day he was supposed to officially retire. His funeral had been heaving and three fights broke out between detectives and reporters who had broken cases they were working on.

'Them dramas on the telly are all about the twists and shocks, but in real life, people do horrible things for the most obvious of reasons,' he told me once. 'No matter how complicated a case seems, boil it down to the basics and follow it along to the logical conclusion.' He'd belched and I got a whiff of the smoky peat of his whisky that made my eyes water. 'Keep focussed on logic. If someone is making a song and dance to get you to look in one direction, it will serve you very well to look in the other.'

'Ellie.'

I had run to Johan's without even noticing. He was just about to open the front door, a cloth bag of groceries under his arm, when he spotted me.

'What happened to your cheek? Are you okay?'

I touched my cheek instinctively. It felt hot around the bandage. 'I'm fine, it was — it was an icicle.' That was true, strictly speaking.

Johan came closer and inspected the dressing, touched it gently. He had been a nurse for several years before Mia got him fired. They had offered him his job back, but he had decided to stay working at the bank for the time being.

'The dressing needs changed,' he said critically. 'You shouldn't go running with fresh stitches. I will fix it.'

HOURS LATER I WOKE. The shadows were long across the floor and I could feel Johan's breath hot against the back of my neck, his arm heavy around my waist. He had changed my dressing gently, expertly as I muttered as succinct an account of the night before as possible.

'You were alone in the dark with him?' he'd asked, his voice curiously formal. He was dabbing antiseptic cream on my cheek, watching his work intently, so I couldn't quite see his expression without crossing my eyes.

'Yeah, but —'

'Ellie, what if he had —'

'But I didn't,' I'd grinned, affecting a cheer I didn't feel. I could feel something uncomfortably trembly deep inside my stomach, but I was fairly confident that my smile remained steady. 'I'm right as rain, give or take a few stitches.'

'Ellie —'

'I don't think he was going to,' I cut him off quickly. 'Hurt me, I mean. He had every opportunity. We were up there alone in the pitch dark, but he chose to run away instead. I got a fright when I saw him there, of course, but I don't think I felt a true, deep threat. I'm not sure I would have chased him if I had. There was something fundamentally cowardly about him.' I yawned.

'Could he still be right about Lotta Berglund? According to the news report he was only charged with the murder of his ex wife.'

'It's possible,' I said carefully.

'But you don't believe it.'

He finished with the dressing then, and led me to the bed, tucked me up with a gentleness that brought a lump to my throat. 'I don't think I do,' I said slowly. 'But I don't know. It's frustrating, but I just don't know. I feel as though I have to start again from the beginning.'

'Then that's what we'll do,' he said softly, and I fell into a deep sleep.

26

The next evening, Johan took my hand as we left the cinema and stepped out into the cold. I was still feeling a bit woozy, so I'd had a quiet day while he was at work, scribbling up my notes from the past few days and starting to form them into something that might eventually make sense. There was something soothing about writing it all down, simply recording the events as they had happened. I'd start puzzling again the next day, but the rest had done my little brain the power of good.

We'd watched a Swedish film, a pleasantly mindless screwball comedy that even I managed to follow the basics of. A shared tub of popcorn and bag of pic 'n mix, which Johan insisted on calling 'small candies' even though they were entirely standard sized sweets, and the horror of the night before receded more than you'd think.

It's a bizarre thing, living through something so enormous, so extraordinary and yet also eating toast and going to the cinema. A little part of my mind was tied up in what possessed Ola Andersson to accuse his ex girlfriend, with flashes of Mattias Eklund's blue-tinged face, even memories of the skeleton that had been all that remained of Sanna, and yet I could also order coffees and be annoyed when I left my season travelcard at home and had to buy a more expensive day ticket. I supposed that was all you could do. Just sort of crack on and hope you don't get murdered.

Now, as we turned up Åsögatan towards his flat, Johan put his arm around me. I snuggled into the soft wool of his winter coat as he did an absolutely shocking impression of the lead actor in the film and I snorted with laughter.

I felt my phone buzz in my pocket with a text and reluctantly pulled my glove off to read it. It was from Corinna.

I had met her back in the summer. Through Mia. We'd got chatting at a dinner Mia had arranged to celebrate the launch of some product or other, and she ended up sending me in the direction of the wife of one of the suspected victims — who had since herself died in questionable circumstances.

Can we talk? Are you free now?

'Tove's mother found these a few days ago,' Corinna explained an hour or so later. We'd nabbed a little table in the corner of the small bar, next to the steamed up window. It was cosy but stuffy. I'd taken off about seven layers and still felt as though I were being slowly poached alive. The bar had some kind of Moroccan tavern theme going on. There was a tassel from the cushion I was sitting on digging into my bum as I looked through the photos on Corinna's phone.

'Tove must have taken them on an actual camera, then uploaded them onto her mother's laptop sometime before she died,' Corinna said. 'They were in a folder marked *abcde* inside another folder of holiday photos, so she never noticed it until she got a new laptop last week and went through the old one to decide what to transfer over. Even then, she didn't think they were important, but a few of us from Tove's office have been visiting her now and then. She mentioned it to us today.'

Tove Svensson had been married to Björne Svensson, a young man who had suffered from chronic pain. His death was initially declared an accidental overdose of painkillers, but Tove refused to accept that, and continued to ask questions until she too died in a car crash having taken a sleeping pill before getting behind the wheel. In the course of her investigation she had discovered that a woman had befriended Björne shortly before his death, but Tove had never managed to identify her.

I had believed it to be Mia.

The pictures on Corinna's phone were of a woman walking down a road somewhere in Stockholm. There were dozens, apparently taken seconds apart. They reminded me a little of the kind you see on celebrity gossip sites that I obviously never visit, that always strike me as spectacularly pointless. Actual gossip I'm all over, but what would I want with a billion pictures of some actor walking along a road with a caption specifying that he is wearing jeans an a T shirt?

'Do you think this is the woman Tove was searching for?' Johan asked.

Corinna shrugged. 'It must be. I don't know why Tove never told anyone she had these. Maybe she did not get the chance.'

Although Tove's mother had no idea when they appeared on her laptop, given that there was no snow on the ground they certainly hadn't been taken in the past few months. The dullness of the light suggested autumn or spring. Most of the photos were taken from behind, then some from a little to the side, as though the photographer had run along the opposite pavement to overtake her and catch her face. She wore a light grey coat that was pinched at the waist, and black leather knee-high boots.

'Do you recognise the road?' I asked Johan, passing him the phone.

He pinched to zoom, frowning intently. 'I think it could be Malmgårdsvägen,' he said finally. 'There is a little bit of a cottage here, maybe, and part of a tree. It is at the bottom of Vitabergsparken,' he added to me.

I nodded. I knew the road he meant, I'd run along it a few times.

'How do we begin to find out who she is?' he asked me. He was trying to keep his voice steady, but I could hear the hope dancing in it, and I knew why.

It wasn't Mia.

The woman in the pictures was shorter, curvier, her stride entirely different. I reached the final photo in the set, in which the photographer had finally managed to get enough ahead of her to grab a shot of her face before she disappeared around the corner.

'We don't have to,' I said. 'I know who that is.'

It was Lotta Berglund.

27

She did not like things that could not be undone. It wasn't fair. On some days, she would never do the things that seemed natural, obvious even, on others. Yet she was expected to account for who she had been on quite a different day.

Often she would say or do something on one day, and on the following day not feel that way at all any more, and yet those around her still gazed at her with suspicion and silence and judgement. It was just one more reason to hate people. Their lack of imagination.

Even Lisbet, who really ought to have known better, banned her from seeing the little girl ever again after she caught her sister pinching the baby when she was just a few months old. Not hard, the girl was barely even crying, and she hadn't intended to hurt her. It was just that those little pudgy arms were so intriguingly fragile looking. Then Lisbet started screaming and she could never make them all understand that now she had done it once she never needed to do it again. Lisbet died soon afterwards so it really didn't matter in the end, but the memory still rankled.

Somebody, one of the teachers or doctors or social workers, had once tried to explain the concept of consequences to her. That words and actions meant something to other people, and would not always be forgiven or forgotten just because the moment had passed. She hadn't been particularly interested at the time and couldn't see what it had to do with her, but now she was a little bit curious about the potential consequences of what was happening now.

The storm she had started.

The storm that had begun to grow beyond her, to include other people. That was the bit that was simultaneously exciting and frightening. She could see it in the others' eyes. Understanding was dawning all around her, tiny invisible synapses connecting to her and how she saw the world.

She had lived many years without ever experiencing connection to other people, and it was an odd sensation, like stepping into a bath she expected to be warm only to find it stone cold. She didn't mind a cold bath, she had had many of them. She just liked to know what she was stepping into beforehand.

28

'It was the same old bullshit.' Anki Manheim had short dark hair in a sleek bob and wore thick, seventies style glasses. She sat back in her desk chair, pressing her fingertips together, looking all the world like an inspiring photo of a female scientist in a school career brochure. Though we must be the same age, give or take, something about her made me feel a little like a naughty school girl called up in front of a stern headmistress.

'How do you mean?'

She sat forward and stared at me intently. 'Well, it is like this,' she said tartly. 'When a team of scientists comprised entirely or primarily of men report results, they are accepted. There is of course a rigorous process of peer review, but it operates within the context that we are scrutinising the results of work that is fundamentally sound. However, when the findings are from teams that are comprised entirely or primarily of women, they are subjected to an endless round of defending not only their conclusions, but the most basic aspects of their process. At best, it is a gigantic waste of time and at worst it fundamentally undermines the dignity of women as professionals working in the field. Several studies have shown that people unconsciously question work that is presented by women.'

'And you believe this is what happened to Lotta's team in Boston?'

'There is no question. She called me close to tears once, recalling how she had been asked to confirm what steps she had taken to ensure that the lab was sterile. It was a level of questioning more suited to an undergrad, and it was humiliating. I don't know whether or not the drug they were working on should have been approved, Lotta herself admitted there was still work to do, but it was this kind of insulting response that made her quit. Not — how did you say that man described it? Like a temper tantrum because she did not get her way? Absolutely not. It was one of the few times I knew Lotta to express vulnerability.'

I nodded as I wrote that down.

'Please do not imagine I am confirming the impression of her put out by that man in the press,' Anki continued, her voice cold. 'The fact is, Lotta is a very contained, reserved person, but this most certainly does not suggest she was capable of cold blooded murder. We live in a society that dismisses women as emotional and weak should we ever betray that we are human, and if we then hide ourselves accordingly we are painted as unfeeling automans who must therefore be capable of the most depraved violence.' Just as I was thinking that Anki herself had a teeny bit of the unfeeling automan about her, her face broke into a grin so sudden I almost jumped. 'Sorry,' she smiled, with an impatient shrug. 'I get a little bit angry when I get going on how women are judged for getting angry. I might not be helping our case.'

'Oh no worries, you are preaching to the choir,' I said,

with more than a touch of relief. 'I've had my sources and data questioned so many times that at one point I took to snapping a rubber band around my wrist to stop me screeching 'do you think I'm a moron' before throwing my skirt over my head and dancing out screaming.

'I knew a woman once, who, every time she was asked to defend her most basic ability to do her job, she would fling her head back and howl like a wolf, then smile and answer the question like nothing had happened.'

'She is my hero,' smiled Anki. 'As is Lotta. Quitting the project and getting on the next flight home the way she did was born of years of that frustration, and in my opinion it took guts. Some would say to stay and fight the bastards, but I understand why she did what she did. Sometimes you know that you are fighting a losing battle. She never responded to a single call or email from anyone associated with the project, she simply said this is not acceptable and she removed herself. After losing her, the project folded. I think in this case, she did the right thing.'

'Based on what you know of the drug she worked on in Boston, could it have been the one used in the murders?'

Anki thought for a moment. 'Yes, it is possible' she said finally. 'Look. I have no evidence to offer you that Lotta is innocent. Nobody can say for certain what they did not witness. None of us even know what those closest to us might be capable of, and I do not even know a Lotta so well. Perhaps she killed these people. But perhaps not. I have not seen any evidence to confirm her guilt, and neither have any of these people calling for her head on a platter.'

'Is anyone doing that?'

Anki rolled her eyes impatiently. 'There is some group of vigilante idiots who announced this morning that they're going to find Lotta and dispense justice because the police are being too slow. They have been patrolling the streets for days claiming they're keeping us safe, when they're probably more dangerous to the general public in the actual killer.'

Don't you want to be safe? The guy with the mournful face and the long hair.

'I think I might have run into them the other day,' I said.

Anki nodded. 'They have been gathering in public places. What the point is I don't know – so they can intimidate any serial killers who happened to be walking past? It is absurd.'

'How do they imagine are going to find Lotta when the police can't?' I asked.

Anki shrugged, rolled her eyes. 'I believe they claim to have inside information, but I doubt it. They are just making noise. They announced this morning that if there is one more murder they will no longer wait for the police, and they will take action themselves. Like some kind of playground threat. I do not imagine there is any real danger from such idiots, but they are consolidating the idea Lotta is guilty in people's minds. They are a danger to her for that reason.'

29

I had promised to cook for Johan, Krister and I, then completely forgotten, so had nipped out for pizza while they watched football.

'I'm not an invalid,' I'd smiled at Johan when he tried to insist on coming with me. 'I've got a bloody cut cheek for heaven's sake.'

And I wasn't an invalid. The break I'd given myself had done me a power of good and I felt more like my old self than I had in a long time. I'd even miraculously managed to remember *utan parmesan*, and though the pizzas were freezing by the time I'd scuttled home through the sub-zero evening with them, I was quite looking forward to mine.

I could hear Johan and Krister laughing and shouting at the screen as, having failed to get three pizzas under one arm to free a hand to open the door, I shoved it open with my shoulder. They sounded normal, roaring at what I vaguely deduced to be a referee's decision they did not agree with.

Krister was looking better too, I thought as I shoved the pizzas in the oven Johan had already heated. There was something a bit less gaunt, less haunted about him. He'd even given me one of his sardonic smiles when I'd confessed to forgetting about dinner. Those smiles used to make me want to stick my tongue out at his smug face, but I was relieved to see one now. Maybe he really was on the mend.

I heard Johan laugh and call something over his shoulder as he came into the kitchen to grab more beers. He kissed the top of my head and ruffled my hair as I stared at the oven in horror, realising that I had managed to bloody burn one of the arsing pizzas.

'Smells good,' Johan grinned, handing me a beer.

'Thanks, I ordered it all by myself.'

I noticed a pile of pamphlets on the counter top. *Don't you want to be safe?* The group of weirdos Anki talked about. The guy who took his life in his hands by trying to get between me and a pastry at Urban Deli.

'You're not involved with this crew, are you?' I asked Johan.

He screwed up his nose, grabbed the pamphlet and chucked it in the bin. 'Of course not,' he said. 'Someone just gave it to me.'

'I was hearing a bit about them. They don't seem like good news.'

'Does your pizza have parmesan on it?'

'No,' I grinned with a level of joy that was somewhat disproportionate. '*Utan* freaking, parmesan, baby.' Johan high-fived me.

It was my pizza that had burned, but it was just the edges and I decided I could pick around the worst of it.

'Did you get pizza salad?' Johan asked.

'Ahh no, I forgot.' I made a face. 'But you're welcome, because nothing pickled has any business being anywhere near pizza.'

'Pizza salad is our greatest invention,' Johan proclaimed as he followed me into the living room. I sat cross legged on the floor by Johan's feet and handed Krister's pizza to him.

'Surely your greatest invention is...' I frowned, pretending to think. 'Weird facial hair? Dynamite?'

'It is the cheese slice,' said Krister.

'The what?'

'The cheese slice. It is a beautiful thing.'

'Do you mean — a knife?' I asked with a grin.

'No, a cheese slice.' Krister swallowed a mouthful of pizza and mimed running something with a handle along a block of cheese. 'Cheese slice,' he said firmly.

'You're making this up. There is no such thing as a utensil specifically for slicing cheese and nothing else. I mean, can it also slice, I don't know, carrots?'

'No it cannot slice carrots.' Krister stared at me in horror. 'Johan, back me up.'

'Dude I have no idea what you are talking about,' Johan said with an almost straight face, and we all burst into giggles.

My phone buzzed with a text and I licked the grease off my fingers as I swiped open it. Corinna again. She had promised to ask Tove's mother if she would meet with me.

She is not so comfortable speaking English but if I am there too to help translate she says okay.

I quickly typed a response saying that was fine, as Johan caught Krister up in Swedish.

'*Va?*' Krister spat.

I felt a nasty twist in my stomach at the venom in his voice. Johan was taken aback too, he almost cowed for an instant, staring at Krister in horror. I shuffled forward a little so that Johan knew I was near.

'What are you playing at Ellie?' Krister turned to me. 'It

was you who discovered what Mia was doing and now you — what? You just change your mind and decide someone else is the killer?'

'Of course not,' I said. 'But if new evidence comes to light then —'

'You are just fucking about with people's lives for fun? Playing detective then changing your mind?'

'It's not like that.'

'Mia is guilty. Mia is a fucking psychopath maniac who murdered Liv. Did you forget that?' he demanded.

Johan flinched as he shook his head.

'Krister, of course we —'

'Why would this Lotta person kill Liv? How would she get into Liv's apartment? No one broke in, remember? Liv let someone she knew in and that person murdered her. Mia.'

'Krister, we don't know exactly —'

'There is not enough evidence —' said Johan, getting to his feet suddenly. His beer toppled over, but he ignored it. 'How can you condemn Mia without stronger evidence?' His voice was tight and strained, and I could see his hands almost straining to form fists.

'We're just asking questions, Krister,' I said quietly.

'Haven't you asked enough questions, Ellie?'

'I am only trying to —'

'Mia is guilty.'

'I don't think she is innocent,' I said. 'I just don't think we know enough about everything that —'

'What the fuck does that even mean?' he demanded.

'Why did you take back your statement about her?' I blurted.

'What? You think a charge of bullying her boyfriend is the main thing the police should focus on about her? She has murdered nine people.'

'Maybe, but taking it back gives the impression that —'

Johan finally spoke again, a stream of rapid, hurt Swedish that I had no hope of following. I sensed him tense up and for a horrible moment was terrified he was going to hit Krister, but he didn't move. Krister shouted back and when Johan replied I caught the word 'Liv' laced with such anguish that it tore at my guts.

'Johan,' I said softly, putting my hand on his arm. I could feel him trembling. 'Guys, let's just —'

'*Fy fan, du vet ingenting*,' burst out Krister. 'You think this woman is guilty because her boyfriend said do? What the fuck does a boyfriend know?'

'There is other possible evidence that —'

'The boyfriend is the last person to know.' He towered over me, ran a hand through his hair, clutched at his head in a way that made my heart break for him. 'How could anyone share a life, share a bed with someone and not know they are a monster?' he pleaded. 'Eat with her, laugh with her, touch her, hold her. Remind her to charge her phone before she leaves for work. It is not possible.'

'Krister —' I got to my feet, reached out to him but he shook me off.

'It is not possible,' he repeated, almost under his breath.

I could hear Johan's upstairs neighbours walking on their creaky floorboards, downstairs' telly. A car roared in too low a gear in some nearby street. The silence in Johan's flat was deafening.

'*Ja vet inte*,' Krister muttered.

'Krister —'

'*Ja vet ingenting.*'

I know nothing.

Johan and I both jumped when the door slammed behind him a few moments later.

30

'Good evening. Thank you very much all of you for coming. I am extremely pleased and proud to see that so many of you share my passion and my belief that we do not have to put up with this. We do not have to cower behind closed doors and glance behind us when we venture out into the darkness. We can stand tall and dignified knowing we have done all we can to keep our community, our friends, our children, our neighbours, safe.'

A little tremor of excitement trembled through her, but she was fairly confident her voice remained steady. She stood at the front of the room – a residents' meeting room in an apartment building where one of the group lived. It was dull and lifeless, painted an industrial beige, the walls adorned with insipid watercolours of flowers. There was a folded up ping-pong table at one end, and a small kitchen area bearing a coffee maker and a tray covered in crumbs that were all that remained of some cardamon rolls an older, stern-looking woman had brought.

And yet it faced with excitement so palpable that she wanted to scream. And she could scream. She might. These were people who would understand. They might even join in. A bolt of sheer thrill rocked through her at the thought of all these people – how many were they, twenty, thirty forty? – all screaming as one. It would be the most real, the most natural thing that had ever happened.

'I am here tonight because I'm angry,' she continued, feeling her voice ring through the gathering. The room was entirely rapt. 'I believe that you are too.' She began to pace at the front of the room, dozens of eyes following her every move.

'Just like you, I bought into society. I paid my taxes, I obeyed the rules. I remove my shoes when I enter someone's home, I take a number to queue for service in a shop, I don't ever drink alcohol before 5pm. And yet I wake one day to learn that a woman, a young beautiful woman with everything to live for, has been murdered? I wake up to learn that none of us are safe in our beds any more?

'And not just murdered, posed like a doll, like a puppet, in the middle of the city where anyone could see, where a child could have found her.' That was good. People always got riled up about the idea of children facing the reality of death, she had discovered, though it was ridiculous of them. She had discussed death many times with the little girl, and the little girl had just nodded silently, staring at her with wide, serious eyes.

'Stripped of every last scrap of humanity. Then just weeks later, a handsome young man in his prime. Who will be next? Will it be the friendly woman who serves you your morning coffee, the kind gentleman who held the door open for you? Or will it be a childhood best friend? Your husband, your child? Who else must die before the police act on information they were given weeks ago – by the killer's own partner. Why do they wait?'

She paused, almost breathless, feeling a rush of unadulterated adrenaline.

'Does nobody else worry that it undermines his accusation that he killed his ex wife?' the woman with the brown eyes had asked earlier. It had been decided early on that they would never exchange names. The woman with the brown eyes used a term that Sigrid had never heard before, plausible deniability. She had repeated it quietly to herself until it sounded comfortable in her mouth. 'We know it is true, but in the eyes of the public? Could it not undermine the righteousness of our mission?'

The man with the little glasses shook his head. 'I don't believe so. There are many examples of couples who kill together —'

'But they didn't —'

He continued as though she hadn't interrupted. 'It is more than established.' He gave a cynical little smile. 'There is someone for everyone, so they say.'

Now, the group seemed to hold their breath as one as Sigrid took her time making eye contact with each person. The stern-looking woman who had brought the pastries was staring at her with a fervour that bordered on religious. The young goth guy, his face covered by painful-looking piercings — when he slipped in she had suspected he had come to make fun of her, but now he was nodding along with her every word. The tense women in the business suit who had clutched desperately her arm with trembling hands when she introduced herself — her eyes were now closed, her expression beatific. As though she could finally rest now that Sigrid was in charge.

'They wait out of fairness to *her*,' Sigrid continued, feeling a collective wave of revulsion rise. 'The killer. They have a sense of duty, of fairness, to the cold-blooded murderer who filled these young, vital people with chemicals and posed them in the snow. They wait because they lack enough evidence to convince the criminal justice system set up to protect the evil. But we will not wait.'

She felt the energy in the room surge, so palpable that she would not have been surprised if a lightbulb had blown. There were a few muted members of agreement, like the distant rumbling of thunder heralding a coming storm. 'We will not protect her,' Sigrid vowed. The rumblings grew, a vibration that thrummed in the air. 'We will not allow her to terrorise our city.'

'No we won't!' shouted a woman, the tense one in the business suit. Her voice was shrill, her eyes widened with the exhilaration of the words escaping her lips.

It was then that Sigrid noticed him. The young man. Thirty, thirty-five perhaps. It had been a long time since Sigrid had been able to judge people's ages. He sat in the very last row. He had been slunk down in his seat, but now he was sitting up straight, staring at her with an expression of wonder. She awarded him with a small smile and was gratified to note that his eyes were shining with tears.

31

'I can't find any other connection between her and Björne Svensson, but there must be a reason that Tove took those photos of her.'

I took a welcome gulp of my red wine, and licked salt off my fingers. When we arrived at the bar an hour or two earlier, Maddie and I had scandalised Lena by ordering a bowl of chips along with our wine.

'But why just French fries?' Lena had asked in confusion. 'If you are hungry you can order a meal.'

'I don't want a meal, I want chips,' I'd explained reasonably.

'Look, if Sweden is going to join the global, you know, world –' Maddie had downed her first glass of red quite quickly – 'you need to get up to speed with the concept of bar snacks. You know I'd really like right now?' she continued with a dreamy expression. 'Nachos.'

Lena's eyes widened in horror.

'Nachos and wine baby.'

'For dinner?'

'No, not for dinner. Along with wine. For no reason.'

Lena frowned now is she thought over the Lotta/Björne connection. 'I suppose if Lotta was having an affair with a married man she would not discuss him at work.' She gave a wry smile. 'And it is even less likely she would have mentioned him to her colleague if she was planning to kill him.'

'When were the photos taken? asked Maddie. 'If it was when Björne was still alive, Tove might have suspected an affair, but if afterwards, it's more likely she suspected Lotta was the killer.

'We don't know,' I said. 'They seem to have been taken with the camera, not a phone.'

'Don't cameras record dates as well?'

'With older cameras you have to set it up. The date on all the photos is the first of the first 1999, which I guess must be the factory setting.'

'Pretty old camera, then.'

'Yeah, I mentioned that to Corinna and she said Tove had been a keen amateur photographer, so she probably had a few cameras.' I sighed. 'The photos certainly create a link between Lotta and Björne and Tove, but what that link means is as clear as mud.

'I keep thinking of this thing an old police contact of mine once told me, that it's always the most straightforward, obvious solution,' I continued. 'But I just can't see any straightforward, obvious solution here, so what is it I'm missing? If Lotta is innocent, then where is she? Why did she take off?'

'There's been no murders since Lotta disappeared,' Maddie said. 'Maybe she is lying low.'

'I may have heard something about her at work today,' Lena said. Lena was a police officer, specialising in cases of domestic violence in another part of the city, but she was friendly with Henrik and Nadja. 'The team who works with technology have discovered that there is a bug in the banking computer system, that maybe creating fake transactions to make it seem as though card is being used when it is not.'

'Henrik told me that Lotta's debit card was used in the Netherlands last week.'

'Exactly. It may not have been.'

'It's pretty high tech to create something that could fool police data media units, surely? Not something any old Joe could do?'

Lena shrugged. 'I suppose.'

'Ola is some kind of developer guy,' I said slowly. 'If somebody faked the transactions in the Netherlands, then it stands to reason they are behind her disappearance. But why would he accuse her so publicly if he hurt her or was holding her hostage? Surely he would either capture her himself or want the world to consider her guilty, but both doesn't add up.'

'Is he the most logical guy though?' asked Maddie dubiously.

I shrugged. 'Yeah that's what Johan said too.' I grabbed the last, little crunchy bit from the chip bowl, and glanced up just in time to catch the look Maddie and Lena exchanged. 'What?'

'Nothing, said Maddie,' a touch too quickly. 'It's good that Johan's getting involved.'

I frowned, looking from one to the other. 'What do you mean?'

'He just seems very interested all of a sudden,' said Lena carefully. 'We only want to —'

'He was worried about me after what happened with Ola,' I said, a little shortly. 'And he wants to find Liv's killer.

He would be thrilled if we manage previous Mia's innocence, but he – he just wants to help.'

'Yeah, as long as —' began Maddie.

Lena cut her off. 'That is good,' she said with a smile I almost bought. 'I think this will need all the brains it can get.'

'Your buddies over in Murder don't quite see it that way,' I said ruefully. 'Nadja nearly took my head off in the hospital. I've been told in no uncertain terms to keep my nose out.'

'Nadja can be a little preoccupied with rules,' Lena smiled. 'Of course she cannot support you doing anything that could put you in danger, and she must be aware of anything that might potentially undermine charges brought, against Lotta, Mia, or, what do you say, Joe Bloggs, that we haven't even thought of yet. But the truth is, as a member of the public you are not subject to the same standard of procedure and chain of evidence that we are. My perspective is that if you can find out who this person is and help to catch them, then we will be safer and that is all that matters. As long as you are safe, of course.'

I felt my smile falter and took a gulp of my wine. For some reason, that night I woke up to find the window open flashed into my mind. But that was my absentmindedness. Third floor. Spiderman. Whoever this person was, they couldn't fly.

'I should probably make a move,' I said as I finished my wine, though the thought of heading back to my weird little empty flat was far from appealing. Maybe I could stay at Johan's, I thought, glancing at my phone. There was no reply to my most recent text to him. I couldn't remember him mentioning any plans for tonight, but he must be up to something. Football-related, probably.

'You reckon that's a first date?' Maddie hissed, too loudly, as we passed a couple at a small table on her way out.

'Yikes,' I grinned.

The guy was leaning back in his chair, arms folded, staring at the woman as the daring her to interest him. She was telling an animated story, seemingly to the candle on the table.

Outside, Maddie linked arms with Lena and I as we made our way to the to T-bana station.

'It is so sad, the guy who died, Mattias-somebody,' Maddie said. 'Seeing that date just now reminded me, I read something about him today. One of his co-workers made a statement describing how excited he was for some Internet date. I know it's silly, but it seems particularly cruel that he never made it.'

'It is worse than that,' Lena said. We paused at the entrance to the T-bana station. 'Mattias Eklund's phone was in his pocket when Ellie found him, so they discovered almost immediately that he had been on his way to a date. Henrik directed a couple of young officers to go to the bar and let her know, but she wasn't there. I believe they have tried to get in contact with her since, but she has not responded.'

'Stood up and murdered on one night? Maddie said mournfully. 'Poor sod.'

'What bar was it?' I asked.

'I'm not sure. One of the pubs on Folkungagatan I think. I'll see if I can find out and text you.'

'Thanks.'

I HUGGED THEM GOODBYE, then cut through Fatburgsparken, across Medborgarplatsen and onto Folkungagatan. There were just a few desultory snowflakes dancing on the breeze here and there, but the wind was bitter, and I stuffed my nose as far into the collar of my coat as I could and still see.

I couldn't help but peer into the cosy, brightly lit bars as I scuttled down the road. A woman who must have been freezing in a black biker jacket opened the door of one as I passed, releasing a blast of warmth and rowdy chatter. I peeked in, wondering about the woman who had stood Mattias Eklund up on the night he died.

I've never been one for Internet dating, not for any snobbish reasons – take it where you can get it, I say – but because it always struck me as somewhat labour-intensive to invest significant text-banter into someone you might not even fancy in person. But most of my friends were on every app going, so I knew that ghosting was hardly uncommon.

'I've only stood somebody up once,' one of the girls from the journalists' night out confided in me once. 'I felt awful, but I spotted him arriving and there were fifteen years and a whole head of hair between his profile picture and the reality. I didn't mind him being bald at all, it was the blatant lie that gave me the creeps. It felt like he'd tricked me, you know? I'd already been on two rubbish dates that week and I just couldn't face one more so I scarpered. I'm not proud, but bloody update your picture, mate.'

The woman who had been due to meet Mattias Eklund must have heard the news surely? I'd have to double check with my friends who used the apps, but I was fairly sure she would have known his real name. The headlines have been dominated by the murders for weeks, and from what Lena had said, it didn't sound as though this woman had come forward.

I was so deep in thought when I got back to the flat that I almost missed the note that had been shoved under the door. It was my general belief that communications that come in the form of paper, unless they are birthday cards containing money, are rarely anything I particularly want to read. I was about to shove it to one side to worry about another day when my eye caught the word *förlåt*. Sorry.

I sighed. This did not bode well. I sat down on the floor and opened my translation app. Moments later, the news I was getting evicted somewhat tempered the triumph of having been able to comprehend that I was getting evicted.

We hadn't bothered with a proper lease when I moved in. Maddie and Lena had warned me against not getting at least some basics in writing, but I'd been so relieved to finally find somewhere that I'd convinced myself it was all sunshine and rainbows and that pesky concepts like 'notice periods' and 'tenants rights' were unnecessarily formal. That was one lesson learned, then.

Of course, I reminded myself as I got to my feet and started peeling off layers, it was also all fine. Johan and I were getting back on track, so it was perfect timing, really. Just as I'd planned.

32

Lena wasn't able to find out which bar Mattias Eklund had been planning to meet his date in, so the next day I set out to tramp the length of Folkungagatan, figuring how many bars could there be on one road. The answer was, a lot.

Small bars, big bars. Trendy bars, sports bars, little old men bars that I guessed hadn't been decorated — or in some cases, cleaned — in forty-odd years. Bars that claimed to be British-themed but as far as I could tell the only actual British thing about them is that they were draped in more Union Jacks than your average angry right-wingers convention. Bars that were probably technically restaurants but when I glanced in I decided they were probably potential date venues so worthwhile checking just in case.

And so far, not one of them remembered a thing about the night Mattias Eklund died. I'd started out at eleven in the morning, figuring that most of them would just be opening so would have time to chat, but I'd forgotten that Swedes have lunch bafflingly early. The lunchtime rush had hit by about half past eleven, so I'd had to give up on a few when I realised that no one would have time to talk to me until later in the afternoon.

I'd now made it to the bottom of Folkungagatan, opposite which was a ferry terminal. An enormous ferry, eight or ten storeys high, sat majestically in the water waiting to go to Finland. Johan had once explained that because the drinks on board those liners are duty free, it's a rite of passage for young Stockholmers who can't afford Swedish bar prices to get wrecked for the first time on a booze cruise across the Baltic Sea. Even if I was a fan of sailing I couldn't think of anything much worse than combining your first hangover with sea sickness. Sure enough, I'd run along the quay where the ferry terminals were enough times to have spotted more than my fair share of pathetically regretful teens deep in the morning-after-the-night-before horrors staggering on to dry land.

It was then that I noticed the sight of the ferry didn't fill me with dread. The night I had had to leap from Krister's boat into pitch dark water to reach the island in hopes of finding the evidence I needed to expose Mia had been a bit of a kill-or-cure moment, but I hadn't had time to really think about it since then. Well that was something, I thought ruefully, as I turned to start tramping back up the hill. The temperature wasn't exactly balmy, but there must have been a bit of a thaw on as there was a decidedly drippy feel to the air. I'd nearly gone flying twice on the steep bit of the hill after stepping on black ice exposed by slushy snow.

I was boiling in my heavy jacket and more than a bit grumpy by the time I made it back up to the Medborgarplatsen end of the road to revisit the bars that had been too busy the first time around. I shoved the door open of the first, and immediately yanked off my sweaty ski hat as the heat of indoors hit me. It was a refreshingly standard bar. No wacky theme; I'd even hazard a guess that all the beers came from mainstream breweries as opposed to organically home brewed by some flinty eyed dude in a remote mountain cabin, who doesn't believe in government or gravity.

There were a couple of older guys nursing pints at the bar, watching what appeared to be a British football match on a wall-mounted screen. A table by the door was occupied by a crowd of punky-goths who seemed to have got lost on their way to 1985.

'*Hej, kan ja hjälpa dig?*' asked the girl behind the bar as I approached. She was early twenties I guessed, possibly a student. She had poker straight dark brown hair that hung half way down her back in a middle parting and enormous brown eyes and porcelain skin that put me in mind of a seventies model. Between her and the punks I was beginning to wonder if I'd accidentally time travelled.

'Hi, sorry, is it okay to speak English?'

She shrugged. I firmly told myself I was imagining the disdain in her expression. I pasted on my most winning, some would say manic, smile.

'Thanks so much. You wouldn't happen to have been working on the third of February, would you? In the evening.'

'I work every night,' she said, as though I had deeply insulted her by suggesting she ever took a night off. 'I am saving to get out of this shithole and move to New York.'

'Right, well, good luck with that.' I pulled out my phone and opened the headshot of Lotta Berglund. 'Do you recognise this woman? Was she in here that evening, by any chance?'

The girl looked at the picture without interest and shrugged again. She shook her head, but I'd seen it. A flicker of nerves. It shot through her eyes and then it was gone, but my heart did a little flip.

'No, sorry.'

'Are you sure? Would you like to look again?'

'I said no.'

There it was again. I leaned forward, pushed my phone towards her. 'Please just look one more time.'

'I think you should go. I can't help you. Maybe she was here that might, maybe she comes in every night to do battle with her liver. I have no idea. It is a pretty busy bar. I don't get time to memorise everybody who comes and goes.'

She finished her tiny speech and stared at me with an expression of fear and irritation that I suddenly realised was directed at me. Damnit. She wasn't harbouring some deep dark secret, she was just shy and resented being put on the spot.

I sighed in frustration. Though things had got better since the summer when I had been deeply grateful for the friendship of a serial killer because everyone else I encountered appeared to hate me on sight, I still often felt as though Swedish social cues were an enigma I might never be able to crack. I'd always prided myself on my ability to read people, to sense if they were friend or foe, lying or truthful. My job rather depended on it, after all, but it appeared that this particular talent ended at the Swedish border.

I belatedly realised that the girl was still staring at me, sending me 'go away' vibes so clear she might as well have unfurled a little *go away* sign from a trumpet and done a *go away* dance complete with high kicks. I turned to leave, then whirled back —

'Look, I'm really sorry if this is inconvenient to you, but a man died that night. A young man at the very beginning of his life. And not just him, nine people have died. Nine people with families and friends who loved them and miss them. And even if some of them didn't have anyone, even if one or two of them were arseholes nobody liked, they did not deserve to lose their lives, so if there is any, teeny-tiny chance that you could possibly know something that might help, why on earth would you not just look at the fucking picture again?'

The girl stared at me, her giant eyes even more deer-like to my headlights, then finally gave one more sullen shrug and held out her hand for my phone. She stared at the picture for a long time, a curious half-frown on her face I couldn't quite read.

'I have never seen her before,' she said at last, handing back my phone. 'I'm sorry.'

'No, it's okay. I'm sorry. I shouldn't have shouted.'

'But if you are wondering about the date of the guy who was killed that night, you will never find her. She does not exist.'

'Excuse me?'

'It was me.' She stared at the bar, refusing to meet my eye. 'I am an actress,' she said in a low voice. 'I trained at Dramaten, but I have not been able to get so much work, but — anyway, it doesn't matter. That is why I am going to New York. But a few weeks ago I saw an ad on a casting website for someone to improvise a phone call pretending to be an internet date. It was two thousand crowns to talk for an hour or two, and at the time, I believed the man on the call was an actor and it was being recorded for some kind of audio drama podcast.

'But then —' she sighed, picked at a bit of black nail

polish that was peeling from her thumbnail. 'There was a short clip on the news the other evening, of the victim, Mattias Eklund, giving some speech or something to his school. I recognised his voice. It was him I spoke to for those two hours.'

33

'Darling this sounds fabulous, I'm loving it all,' said Kate around a mouthful of crisps. The familiar packet gave me a pang of homesickness as she balled it up and tossed it under her desk. You could get salt and vinegar crisps in Sweden, after a fashion, but nothing tastes like the ones you grew up with. 'Terribly sorry, bit hungover and a meeting ran through lunch so if I don't get copious amounts of salt, sugar and caffeine into my system, might die.'

'Please don't die on my account,' I grinned, taking a sip of my tea. Ordering a cup of tea in a Swedish coffee shop and getting anything that remotely resembled a British cup of tea was an exercise in futility and heartbreak, I'd discovered. However, through a bit of trial and error, I had come across a herbal one called Söderblandning, which, with no milk and a splodge of honey, turned out to be more than palatable.

I was in the café near Johan's flat with all the mismatched furniture where the newcomers group normally met. Today though, it was full of freelancers typing silently on laptops and one group crowded around a table in the centre who, judging by their running shoes and loud voices, were American tourists. They were oblivious to the death stares their lively chat was garnering.

My publisher had asked for a quick web call to catch up on how things were going with the book. I still had a while before I had to turn the first draft in, 'but with it being a live case, as it were,' Kate had explained, 'its nice to stay on top of how it's all going so that I'm prepared in case anything changes.

'What I really want to do quite soon,' she said now, opening a chocolate biscuit. 'Is start getting a bit of heat going, you know? Nothing too specific, just get it on the radar, start building anticipation.'

'But how are you going to do that when we don't know the story yet?' I asked.

'Just like I said. It's Scandi, there's murder and it's true. Job done, tickety boo. The fact it's live and ongoing just makes it all the more thrilling. In fact,' she added, tapping her chin thoughtfully as she chewed her chocolate biscuit. 'Playing up the element of you being in danger could really make it sing. You know, you don't know who the killer is but they know you, kind of thing. Sorry!' she grinned, apparently catching my expression. 'Quite sure you're not in any danger of course. You'd better not be, in fact, I don't have budget to hire another writer if you're not around to finish it.'

I laughed, a touch too merrily, as I thought of my open window. The night before, I'd half woken from a deep sleep sometime in the wee hours, and for an instant had thought that the window was open again. Goosebumps prickled over the back of my neck as I stared into the unrelenting darkness, afraid to move a muscle in case I disturbed the monster under my bed. Except, obviously, that there was no monster under my bed, because I was on an air mattress on the floor. And also, I was an adult.

The window wasn't open, of course, I had just imagined it in that hazy state between sleep and consciousness. Little nerves darted in my guts as I strained my ears, tried desperately to identify what had woken me, what had made me tense up with fear. A chilling sense that I wasn't alone.

A bad dream. Obviously. In the light of day it was laughable. I couldn't remember anything of the dream, but it must have been a whopper, I'd thought in the morning, rolling my eyes at myself for being such a plonker.

'Your budget is safe with me,' I grinned. 'There is no denying the killer has gone quiet since Lotta Berglund disappeared, and the police have now discovered that the first victim, Anna Essen, was also on her way to meet an internet date. She was really secretive about being on a dating app, maybe because she was semi internet famous herself, so she had an unregistered burner phone for it that they've only just found.'

'Interesting. Those things are like bloody menus to predators,' Kate said, shaking her head. 'I've just found out that my fifteen year old daughter wants to go on them, and I told her not on my watch, my darling. You'll sneak into a club and snog the first spotty youth to grind up against you, like a normal teenager, thank you very much.'

'They've put calls out to try to discover if a male actor was hired to pretend to be her date, but no one has come forward so far,' I added. 'The girl I met in the bar had no idea who hired her. The whole thing done by email and bank transfer and they've had no luck yet tracing any communications she had. Dummy servers and all that.'

I'd set up a couple of profiles on the dating app that Anna Essen and Mattias Eklund had used, one a woman looking for men and another a man looking for women. I wasn't really expecting to come across a profile picture with crazy eyes and a bio asking how good you were at musical statues, but I swiped through whenever I got a chance. It had been a good couple of weeks since Mattias Ekland's death; if the killer was still at large, they must have been getting antsy by now.

So far, all I had encountered was so many torso shots from men and duck faces from women that I wondered if the app's tagline was *I have abs and you have lips. Let's fall in love!* I'd come across one photo of a guy with a paper bag on his head and a somewhat pious little blurb underneath imploring women not to judge him by his looks. Which was all fine and good, but the nature of apps is that that the only information they therefore had about him was the fact that he used paper and not plastic. Call me shallow, but I'd like a little more to go on when choosing a romantic partner. There was also one guy whose profile picture was a toy frog, which I'd hesitated on a moment, lip curling a tiny bit with distaste. There was something gross about using what was presumably your child's toy to pick up women. A moment later, something had made me want to look at the frog again, but it turns out that once you've swiped someone away, they are forever gone.

'This killer, whoever they are, is good at what they do,' I said now, snapping my thoughts back to the meeting with Kate. 'That's the only thing that links these two murders to the earlier ones. They're like, I don't know, a great white shark or something, they way they kill and cover up their tracks so flawlessly.'

'I've seen great whites kill on holiday in South Africa, and there's nothing subtle about it at all, my darling. Bloody sea was red for miles around, it seemed.'

'Bad reference,' I smiled, 'though I'm sure I've heard some nature documentary refer to great whites as killing machines.'

'Yes, I do know what you mean,' Kate said. Someone handed her a cup of tea and she flashed a grateful smile over the monitor.

'What I wouldn't do for a British cup of tea right now,' I grinned mournfully. 'I've run out of teabags and my mum keeps forgetting to post more.'

'I'll post you some,' Kate promised. 'Can't expect a writer to exist on anything less than a constant drip of caffeine.'

'I'm not sure about announcing anything yet,' I blurted, before I could lose my nerve. 'I just — could you give me a little more time? I just have this sense that there's — I don't know. Something big I'm missing, or misunderstanding. I'm sorry, I could be wrong, I just —'

'Tell you what,' said Kate. 'There's a book fair coming up in three weeks. I'd like to say something about this then. How does that sound?'

'Three weeks is fine,' I said, affecting a confidence I didn't feel. 'I'll definitely be on the right track by then.'

34

Lotta Bergland opened her eyes and horror rushed over her like a tidal wave. A scream caught in her throat and for a moment she thought it would choke her. She sat up, wracked with a coughing fit as she fought to breathe through the terror before it drowned her.

This happened every time she opened her eyes. For the first few days, she had carefully scratched her arm with the rusty edge of the metal bed frame every time she woke up. Gritting her teeth against the pain, she'd reminded herself over and over that she didn't need to draw blood. She would be rescued long before the shallow scratches healed. It was just a little ritual that would help ground her, keep her connected with reality, with the passage of time, stop her from losing her mind.

She now had no idea how long she had been held in the pitch darkness for. After she had scratched herself all the way up to the elbow, she had run her fingers over the tiny cuts, feeling the tiny scabs here and there from when she had accidentally cut too deep. She had counted seventeen scratches. But that wasn't possible. She couldn't have been here for seventeen days.

She couldn't have lasted that long on a few sips of stale water and knäckbröd that had gone soft and very possibly mouldy. She was aching, she felt nauseated with fear and exhaustion and disorientation, and her head had pounded now for as long as she could remember, but she did not feel truly malnourished or even dehydrated. She had passed a few hours trying to recall as much as she could from a pre-med class she had taken as an undergrad before deciding that dealing with laymen's attempts to describe their symptoms on a daily basis would drive her out of her mind.

Dehydration would kick in first, of course.

Increased thirst. She certainly had that, but she would feel thirsty after just a few hours with less water than usual, so that was no cause for concern.

Dry mouth. Similarly, she had experienced dry mouth after running in warm weather. Nothing to worry about.

Tired or sleepy. She was certainly sleeping a lot, but that could also be down to decreased serotonin production from being in the darkness for so long.

Headache. She had that, but again there could be several possible reasons for this.

Dry skin. Lotta had always been prone to oily skin and had suffered from debilitating acne as a teenager. She had often wondered if she would have had the opportunity to develop better social skills had she not spent her teenage years hiding her face from everyone. Regardless, it was not particularly dry now.

Extreme dizziness or lightheadedness. Not extreme.

Rapid heart rate. No more than terror would account for.

Fever. Definitely not. She would almost welcome fever. There must be some kind of heating source in this building, whatever it was, as she would have died from a night, possibly two at most, of outdoor temperatures. However it certainly was not a cosily insulated and central heated residence, and she was aching partly from curling in the foetal position as much as possible in an instinctive effort to protect her internal organs from the chill.

She could not, therefore, have been without a reasonable amount of water for more than two or three days. That was when she realised she must have been dosing on and off and scratching herself several times throughout each day. So she she had no means of knowing how much time had passed.

The abyss of terror rose up and she forced herself to sing out loud to beat it back before it could claim her. She had no idea until now that she knew so many songs. Ridiculous pop songs she must have heard from colleagues' radios over the years. Midsummer drinking songs. Nursery rhymes half-remembered from long ago daycare.

Every once in a while she forced herself to get out of the bed and carefully feel her way around the room. She was reminded of an old black and white film she had seen once in which an actress walked around a room, touching the curtains of the four poster bed, the tapestries on the walls, the carved wooden furniture. When asked why, she explained that in the future she would live in this room a great deal in her memory.

Lotta sincerely hoped that she would never again return to this room in her memory or in any other way. She was searching for some clue that would give a hint as to where she was, what sort of building. Whether there was a door that could somehow be forced open. A window or a vent that could be screamed through.

A weapon.

She could only hope that she might get the opportunity to use a weapon.

She had never believed in Stockholm Syndrome before, but she was fairly sure that should a human being ever open the door, she would fall to her knees and worship them. Whoever they were. Whatever they planned to do to her.

Her throat started to close up again as torturous images flashed at her of things they might do to her. Would that be better or worse than being locked in here forever to slowly die? Her breathing shortened, became shallow, desperate, as she reminded — or perhaps instructed — herself, over and over, that she would lose consciousness from dehydration long before she lost her mind from being buried alive.

Ola must have noticed her absence, she thought desperately as she closed her eyes and tried to count her breaths. Her few acquaintances from work may well still be assuming that she had just decided to work from home for a few days. Her family knew not to expect to hear from her for weeks at a time. This was one way to learn a lesson about maintaining a social life outside of work, she thought, and a harsh bark of laughter that didn't sound anything like her, shattered the silence.

But she and Ola had been sleeping together long enough that he wouldn't expect she would just drop contact with no warning, she hoped. She had reminded him many times not to count on her, not to expect anything from her, but even if he assumed himself dumped, he wouldn't just accept that. He would show up at her apartment building and bang incessantly on the door until her neighbours complained, or march through her office shouting for her. Then someone — Anki, maybe — would confront him, tell him to go home, but somehow in the ensuing conversation it would be established that no one had seen her in several days and then maybe, hopefully, someone would raise the alarm.

She knew she was not supposed to enjoy Ola's bullying ways. She had listened in to enough of her female colleague's conversations to be fully aware that a an acceptable romantic partner was expected to respect boundaries, admire independence. But after so many years of — admittedly self-imposed, but still — isolation from any real human entanglement, the way that Ola declared his possession of her thrilled her.

And now she could only pray that it would save her.

At the thought that he might have taken her at her word, might believe that she had simply dropped him and so she would be left here to rot forever, the terror rose up and this time she couldn't beat it back.

She closed her eyes and sang desperately into the darkness.

Ja må hon leva, ja må hon leva, ja må hon leva uti hundrade år.

Yes, may she live for a hundred years. Or at least another hundred hours, Lotta thought ruefully. Just long enough for Ola to raise the alarm.

35

Tove Svensson's mother lived in a small, neat house at the edge of a suburb in Northern Stockholm. I stood by the patio doors and stared out at the wild afternoon as Maria brewed coffee for us both. It was lashing down with rain on top of snow, which was a level of weather misery I had never even considered. I'd waded through ankle-deep slush from the train station, and now my boots and socks were steaming on Maria's bathroom radiator.

'Here is a pair of socks you can wear for now,' Maria said softly, handing me a thick pair of hand-knitted, bright red socks. Something about them was so cheerful, so assured of happy Christmases and cosy winter evenings, so at odds with the haunted woman who scuttled back to the kitchen as the coffee maker beeped that I felt a wave of melancholy sweep over me.

Maria was a small, neat woman, much like her house, with wispy hair held back in a clip and sensible, nondescript clothes. The devastation that swam in her eyes even as she smiled and, in hesitant English, politely invited me in was heart wrenching. Corinna had texted to say she had been held up. She had suggested I wait at the train station, but by the time I noticed the text I was half way up the pavement of slush, so I just pressed on.

'Tove was very beautiful, wasn't she?' Maria said, handing me a coffee. She put a plate of biscuits on a little side table next to be, but though I was hungry it didn't feel right to crunch away in the midst of this woman's grief. Her eyes shone with tears as she gazed up at the wall that was covered with photographs of her daughter, from chubby grinning baby, through awkward school shots to serious young woman who was, indisputably, beautiful.

The largest photo was of Tove and Björne's wedding day. Tove wore a simple white shift dress, Björne handsome in a grey suit. They weren't posing formally, but grinning wildly, arms wrapped around one another, cheeks smooshed together with expressions of such unadulterated joy that I had to look away.

'They were so happy that day,' Maria said, following my gaze. 'Of course, one hopes that everyone is happy on their wedding day, but so often persons get caught up in the stress of flowers and caterers and many things that does not matter.'

Maria's English was definitely a little shakier than, say, Johan's, but it was a lot better than Corinna seemed to think. Corinna had impressed on me several times that Maria would be much too shy to speak to me, but with the odd hesitation as she sought for words, she seemed to be managing just fine.

'Tove and Björne did not care about any of that. There was no flowers, they forgot to order them in the beginning. They was just so happy to be together at last.'

'That's lovely,' I said. 'That's how it should be, I think.'

'Mmm,' Maria nodded eagerly. 'Tove was so in love with

him since she was a child, but it was a stupid boy and did not notice. So she went away to travel the world to try to forget him. As soon as she came home he proposed.'

'Good for him.'

'The night before the wedding, she told me that she did not go away to try to forget him, but to teach him what his life was like without her. She knew that he would learn what she had known since they were fifteen years old. Tove was — what do you say, she was not arrogant, but — she was very certain of things. She was quite sure of what she was worth, to Björne, to her employers, her friends.' Maria smiled, her eyes far away. 'I hope I helped her to grow that confidence.

'But after Björne died, it was as though her faith in everything and everyone just disappeared. Her sense of justice, of right and wrong —' Maria shook her head. 'They kept telling her that he had killed himself, either as an accident or on purpose. She knew that was not true, and those two things —' Maria waved her hands up and down in opposite directions to suggest conflict. 'It shattered her world.'

'Maria, do you believe that —'

We were interrupted by a sharp knock. Corinna was here. My heart sank. I knew she was only trying to help, but it was important that I got Maria's impressions and memories first hand as much as possible, in her own words.

'Hi, I am so sorry, the train just sat at Ulriksdal for a million years and they did not even explain why. I thought maybe you would be on it too?'

Corinna grabbed one of the biscuits as she sat next to me on the sofa. I could hear Maria bustling away in the kitchen and I had a mad impulse to dash in and lock Corinna out so I could talk to her a little more.

'I must have got the one just before.'

'*Oh! Tusen tack Maria,*' Corinna gushed as Maria handed her a coffee. She then continued chatting in Swedish, so rapidly I was quickly hopelessly lost, so I sipped my own coffee and tried not to be too annoyed.

The language issue is an odd one in Sweden. On the one hand, in principle, of course us newbies should make every effort to speak Swedish. I could only imagine the outcry if French people moved to London and went around asking everyone if they could speak French for their convenience. However, on the other hand, they all speak fluent English and I do not speak fluent Swedish, so there's an inherent imbalance. I knew it wasn't reasonable to find it rude for people to speak their native language in their own country just because it meant I had to sit there like a lemon, but on the other hand, it was a bit rude.

Based on what little I could pick up of their conversation, I gathered that they had strayed from the subject altogether and decided not to fight it for a moment. I scrolled though my phone and noticed a text from Lena. *Just heard that Anna Essen told a friend her date the night she was murdered was American.*

American. Boston? It wasn't impossible that a Swedish actor had been hired to talk to her and had put on an accent. But, *always the most straightforward solution*. Odds were, Anna Essen had spoken to an actual American. The Boston murder, I was increasingly certain, was key.

'We had just started to talk about how Tove changed after Björne's death,' I butted in.

'Of course, sorry Ellie,' Corinna smiled.

'Yes, it was hard for her because —' Maria began, but Corinna cut her off with something in Swedish.

'She says that it was difficult for Tove because she was so

certain all along that Björne would never have deliberately or accidentally taken the overdose, but no one would believe her.'

'Yes, we had already got that far.' I did my best to keep my impatience out my voice, but Corinna didn't seem to notice. It continued like that, with Corinna asking questions then translating vague, basic platitudes about how difficult Björne's death was on Tove.

'I'm interested in the last few times that Tove visited,' I broke through another stream of Swedish. 'Could you ask her about those? Did Tove ask to use her laptop at any time, or disappear with it?'

Maria shook her head slowly, frowning thoughtfully as she tried to remember. Finally she responded, and Corinna turned to me with a triumphant smile. 'The last time Tove came, just three days before her death, she was very preoccupied and worried. Just before she left, she asked if she could check her email on her mother's computer because her phone had run out of battery.'

'Did Maria see Tove use the laptop?'

I glanced over at Maria as I asked, feeling daft directing the question to Corinna when I knew full well Maria could understand.

'Tove took the laptop into the bedroom to use it,' Corinna translated. 'But Maria remembers her taking something from her purse.'

'Something like a USB stick?'

Corinna nodded. 'Tove uploaded those photos to her mother's laptop and three days later she was dead.'

36

Sigrid had once read a book about how human beings were pack animals. To excel in life and be content, it claimed, one had to function as part of a unit. Co-operation, it explained, was the key to life.

At the time, Sigrid had thought it childish. *Let's all be friends together*. It was the sort of thing that the teachers and doctors and social workers used to say to her, and even as a child she had found it ridiculous.

'Try to think of others,' a teacher had once pleaded. Sigrid had eaten a classmate's packed lunch, and the girl, whose mother had packed her a slice of cake as a special treat, was howling on the teacher's lap. Sigrid couldn't understand why she was making such a fuss. It was only cake. 'You cannot just help yourself to whatever you want if it belongs to someone else,' the teacher tried again.

'But I wanted it,' Sigrid reasonably explained.

As she got a little older, she began to understand that if she did things for others — or at least did not eat their cake — they would do things for her. She could see the value in that, it was just that when she wanted something, there never seemed to be time to remember that it might upset someone else if she took it. Sigrid learned to accept that she was simply not a pack animal, and she managed perfectly well.

Since all the things had begun to change, however, Sigrid had learned that it could in fact be useful to co-operate with other people. Sometimes, other people knew things she didn't or had skills she lacked. The idea had never occurred to her before, though once she thought of it, she realised that someone must have figured out how to make airplanes fly or how to turn flour and yeast into bread or fix toilets. Sigrid had no idea how to do any of those things. She had never been on an airplane, but she had eaten bread and used toilets, so she supposed that she owed other people something after all.

And although the storm was gathering around her, although it was she who controlled the people who came to the meetings and she who would decide when it was time, she was willing to admit that the skills some of the others brought had their uses. Things with computers, for example.

She had taken a computer class at school once upon a time, back when they were enormous bulky things with black screens and greenish text. During her first class, Sigrid realised that all the other girls were already typing away while she was still tying to figure out how to open the screen that would allow her to type. It made her furious so she walked out and never touched another one of the stupid things again.

Sigrid had a mobile telephone, that one of the doctors or social workers gave her, but the screen showed only numbers and occasionally text messages from the telephone company telling her to upgrade. Now, however, one of the young men, a skinny one with round little eyeglasses, thin hair held in a scraggly ponytail and skin that always shone with sweat, had given her a box thing he insisted was a phone.

It didn't have any buttons, but a glassy screen she was supposed to touch to make it work. Sigrid had been about to object and throw the thing back in the young man's face, when she decided she liked the feel of the cool glass beneath her fingertips.

The young man swallowed several times as he explained that there was only one box-picture she had to concern herself with. His prominent Adam's apple bounced up and down and Sigrid wanted to jab it with her fingers to see what it felt like, but then she remembered that if she did that, he would probably take the phone away from her. She smiled when she realised that she had learned about consequences at last. That doctor or teacher or social worker would be proud, if they were still alive.

The young man did something to the screen to take all the other box-pictures away, until only the black one with the grey circle remained. He showed Sigrid how to tap it with her finger tip to open a camera image. At first, Sigrid didn't understand what she was seeing. The screen was a sort of lime-green, and to begin with, it made Sigrid's eyes hurt. But as her eyes adjusted, she realised that she could see a person lying on a bed.

The person was curled up, their knees almost to their nose, but Sigrid could see their face twisted with fear and devastation. They were moving their mouth — talking to someone? Shouting? Singing? Sigrid couldn't hear anything, but she could feel the person's terror throb right out of the phone, and her heart started to beat faster.

Then the young man explained that it was her. The killer. And Sigrid could watch her whenever she wanted.

37

'Weirdest fuckin' thing I ever saw in my life,' Marty MacDonald said into the webcam. 'And I saw a lot of fuckin' weird things in my life.'

After emailing what felt like the entire population of Boston, I'd finally reached someone who was willing to talk to me about the Ice Statue Killer. Marty MacDonald had retired from the homicide department three years earlier, and cheerfully confessed over email that he was bored as shit and happy to chat to anyone about anything.

'This is what happens,' he'd groused when I first answered the call. He opened a can of beer and took a healthy swig, even though I was pretty sure it was about 10am in the States. 'They expect you to give up your entire life for the job, so your wife leaves you, kids could hardly pick you out of a line up, buddies don't even remember your name, then retirement comes and boom, you're out and you've got no one. Just gotta spend the rest of your whole life sitting in a chair watching TV.'

'Couldn't you go out and make friends now?' I'd asked. 'Take up bowling or something?'

'Bowling?' He'd stared at me aghast. 'You want me to take up bowling? I've got gout in my left foot and arthritis everywhere else.' He shook his head. 'I try to wind up to shoot and you just watch me fall and slide all the way down the lane after the ball like a possum on ice. Is that what you want for me?'

'Perhaps not bowling, then. Maybe paper maché?'

'What?' In his horror he choked on a mouthful of beer and went into a coughing fit that lasted for several minutes.

'The Ice Statue Killer?' I said when he'd finally recovered.

'Right, sure. Why you want to talk about that now? It was six years ago, ain't gonna be solved.'

'I'm writing a book about unsolved murders,' I said with deliberate vagueness. 'It's an interesting one, so I'd like to include it.'

'It sure is.'

'You worked it, right?'

'Sure did.'

'What would you do differently if you were investigating it starting today?'

He raised his eyebrows, nodded slowly as he thought. 'Well now that's a good question, young lady.'

I took a sip of my tea — Kate had come through on her promise to send me a few boxes of proper builders' teabags — and resisted snapping that I wasn't particularly young, nor was I much of a lady. There wasn't much point in taking my bad mood out on someone who could help, I reminded myself, taking a deep breath to try to release the bad feelings as I'd been taught in a yoga class Maddie dragged me along to. I'd been doing bloody great releasing breaths all morning waiting for it to become a reasonable time to phone Boston, and I still felt like shit.

Johan didn't want me to move back in.

'It's great, Ellie,' he'd said, when I told him I was being chucked out. But it was too late. I'd felt his hesitation. Just for an instant, that flash of uncertainty in his eyes that had sent my heart plummeting, before he smiled and started chatting, too quickly, about helping me to carry my stuff back. He'd never even been here, I thought resentfully, in all these months.

Not that I'd wanted him to. He might have offered to visit once or twice in the first couple of weeks in fairness, but I'd not really wanted him to see my weird little indoor camping lifestyle so I'd put him off, but still.

Okay, now I thought about it, that bit was on me.

But he had definitely hesitated about me moving back, and right now I just didn't know what to do with that. Was it too late? Had we died the moment I moved out, and I'd just been kidding myself all this time that it was possible to go back a couple level and then move forward again? The thought of it being over, of us just not being together again at all, sent a great swirling mass of misery over me, but —

But he had hesitated.

'I would have taken more time to strategise,' Marty MacDonald said, and I nearly jumped. 'You gotta understand, the Winslow family are big people around here. Jason's old man is country club buddies with my commissioner, so the directive from on high was to solve it, and solve it fast. Problem is, sometimes a case just takes a bit of time. There was pressure to be seen to be taking all the action, so we were out there visibly interviewing just about every goddamn person who stepped foot on a twenty block radius of the crime scene in their whole lives. So what we ended up with was a huge mass of statements from people who didn't know a thing and wasted time sifting through all of those. I don't know what we missed in that time we wasted, but I know we missed something.'

'Did you ever have focus on a particular suspect?'

'Not really, to tell the truth. It was crazy. I don't know how much you already know about it, but you need to realise that Jason Winslow was about the last person you ever would expect to be a murder victim. I know it's not all PC to profile folks these days, but reality is what it is. White, six foot four, male athletes are not a demographic I lose a lot of sleep worrying about getting murdered, you know what I mean?

'But that was the problem.' He shifted in his easy chair, grimacing. 'It made us look for a personal motive. Somebody with a grudge against him, his family. The freaky way the body was embalmed and posed suggested serial killer, but it just didn't figure he was a random victim. I mean, I'm a serial killer and I walk down a street filled with a bunch of cute little co-eds I could snap with one hand, and I pick the guy on the starting line up of a top league basketball team? It just doesn't make sense.

'Now though, I've got nothing but time to think, and I reckon that's exactly what it was. I've got a criminal profiler buddy, we drink from time to time when he's in town. We talked about this case a little, it's one those of us who were around won't ever forget. I think this guy killed the most unlikely victim to make a point. Something about proving his power, his superiority. He wasn't just some run of the mill bad guy who strangled a hooker, right?'

I cringed at the casualness with which he said 'strangled a hooker,' but I knew what he meant. The showiness of these murders was key. It always had been. This killer wanted us to notice them.

'You said guy,' I pointed out.

'What's that?'

'The killer. You think it was definitely a man?'

Marty MacDonald chuckled. 'Look, I'm all for women's lib, lady. Have your career, don't make me a sandwich, I don't care. But don't waste your time looking for a female here. Aside from the fact that women just don't typically murder in this kind of way — they don't make movies about lady killers not because they don't exist, but because they don't kill in popcorn-friendly ways. They poison, most often and that can be subtle, sometimes the victim dies a week later. There are less lady serial killers, but statistically they are more successful, if you wanna think of it like that, because they keep it on the down low. They tend to be at large for a lot longer than men who eventually stop being so careful.'

'This killer was successful,' I pointed out. 'Six years later and you have no idea who they are. Maybe they are a woman, then.'

'Honey, even if I believed a woman had a mind that sick, Jason Winslow was six foot four with pecs the size of my head. If a woman carried his dead body, she was a freak of nature.'

AN HOUR OR TWO LATER, I was sorting through the random bits I'd accumulated over the past few months in a vague, reluctant attempt to stat packing. I could have sworn I'd not bought a thing, and yet my stuff was suddenly about three times bigger than the suitcases I'd brought it in. I was going to have to acquire a new bag, or box, or something to move to — wherever I was going to move to.

I felt as though lead was dripping through my veins. The thaw had been on for days, and though the winter wonderland had somewhat outstayed its welcome, I'd chose it any day over the unrelenting greyness the city was melting into now. Rain was battering ceaselessly against the window. I chucked the jumper I'd been in the middle of folding on the floor and threw myself onto the air mattress, lay staring at the ceiling.

I was not going to cry. Feeling sorry for myself was not an option. I didn't have time, and more importantly, if I gave into it now, I was far from certain I would have the energy to ever pull myself back out.

I started to picture just living the rest of my life just crying my eyes out, and a smile tugged at my lips. Having brunch with friends, tears streaming down my face. Taking a tap dancing class, howling with misery. Getting married, shuddering with sobs.

Yeah, I'd maybe keep that one as Plan B.

I grabbed my phone, thinking that mindless session of funny cat videos might be just the ticket, when I noticed an email had just come through from Marty MacDonald.

This is technically a live case but I'm retired and don't give a damn. Just to give you an idea of the stupid scale of this investigation, I found a list of every witness we interviewed. Maybe you'll see how we never had a chance.

Stifling a yawn, I opened the attachment and scanned the list of names. Sure enough, there were dozens and dozens. Next to each name was a code with a hyperlink, that presumably connected to the person's statement. I clicked on a random one, but came up against a screen asking for my credentials, so I navigated back to the list.

There wasn't much I could do with a list of names, I thought, other than reassure Marty MacDonald that it wasn't his fault the case was never solved. Then I noticed one that made me sit up straight.

Lotta Berglund.

Lotta Berglund hadn't just been in the same city when the murder took place, she had been interviewed by police. She had been based at Harvard, and the body was found in a small park at the edge of the Charles River just a few blocks from Harvard's campus, I reminded myself. Marty MacDonald had been quite clear that they had interviewed pretty much anyone who had ever been in the vicinity, so it very possibly meant absolutely nothing that she was on the list.

I fired off a quick message to Marty MacDonald asking what he remembered about her, then returned to the list again.

Which was when I noticed the name below hers. I pulled up an app I hadn't opened in weeks, and was relieved to discover that my login still worked, clearly Sandra was about as up to date on admin as I would have predicted.

I swiped back and forth between the two, heart hammering as I tried to process the impossible. The American Anna Essen had spoken to. And then I remembered the dating app profile. The profile with the stuffed frog.

Koak.

I had got absolutely everything wrong.

38

'Henrik!' I yelled.

It was too mild for the thick snow boots I was wearing and my feet felt as though they were being boiled alive, but it had been too wet and slushy for trainers. I slowed to a walk about a block away from the police station, trying to catch my breath. Neither Henrik nor Nadja had answered their phones and clearly, no amount of running or hellish bootcamps were a match for a wild sprint halfway across Södermalm through half melted snow in heavy boots.

I could see Henrik now, leaning against the police station, hunched over, one foot propped against the wall. I spotted the glow of a cigarette dangling between his fingers, though as I hurried up the pavement as fast as my shaking legs would carry me, he didn't take a single drag. I knew someone once who'd given up smoking years ago, but lit up every once in a while just to feel it, inhale the sharp, acrid scent, only to then stub it out with a little self-congratulatory smile.

'Yeah, closest I had my eye on anyone it was Casey

Donnantuoro,' Marty MacDonald said a few moments ago when I got hold of him again. I refrained from reminding him that he'd told me there was never a particular suspect in the frame not an hour earlier. 'But there was just nothing strong enough to stick, save for him being a weirdo. And a trainee coroner at the time, so he would have known his way around a post mortem. There was no connection we could find whatsoever between him and Jason Winslow, and like I said, we were looking for a personal motive.'

'Henrik —' I said again as I approached him, but he didn't respond. Did he have earphones in or something, I wondered. His hood was pulled low over his face, and it crossed my mind that standing out here in the rain was a helluva dedication to smoking for a man who hadn't taken a single drag in several minutes. I glanced down at the cigarette in his hand and saw that it had burned right down to the stub. The orange glow was directly between his fingers, the skin touching it blackened.

'Henrik? No, no — Henrik —'

I didn't even realise I was screaming until people came running.

39

'Casey Donnantuoro wife is protecting him,' Nadja said. 'Somehow he got wind we were coming to arrest him and he ran. I think she knows where he is but she will not say.'

I had been sitting on a hard plastic seat in the reception area of the police station for most of the night, watching the muted, stunned commotion as the news spread that one of their own had been killed. Sometime in those first few moments, an ashen-faced officer had led me in here, got me a coffee, promised me that a statement would be taken soon.

Hours had ticked by. I'd refilled the coffee so many times I could feel every cell jittering. I felt numb, detached almost. As though I were in a nightmare, experiencing what felt real, but aware on some level that it couldn't possibly be real. I supposed I was free to go, but I couldn't bring myself to stand up and leave.

Finally, sometime in the small hours, Nadja had come in and slumped into the chair next to me. She'd sat in silence for several moments, grief emanating from her almost like a physical fog. I'd seen her pass to and fro a few times throughout the night, and she had seemed like her normal self, barking out instructions, listening to reports. I'd been in awe of her composure, but now I realised it had all been a front.

'I just don't understand,' she said with a smile that bordered on manic. 'This is a police station. He murdered Henrik right under the noses of Stockholm's police force. Officers have been coming and going all night, passing within metres of the body and nobody noticed.' Her voice was low, but edged with a shrill note of hysteria. I wasn't sure if it was my place to suggest she get herself checked for shock, but I definitely wasn't going to leave her alone.

'How could his wife protect him after what he's done?'

Nadja shrugged with great effort. 'Denial is a powerful thing, I suppose. To accept all we told her tonight, she would have to admit that her entire life has been a lie. The poor woman has that little boy to think of —'

'Tor-Björn,' I said softly, remembering the weight of his little body when he had finally stopped crying and curled up in my arms, sucking on his dummy, as I read him a story.

'And one on the way by the looks of it. It will take her months of therapy to even begin to process it, but I don't know how we will find him in the meantime.' She yawned deeply and rubbed her forehead.

'Based on what we have discovered so far,' she continued, he trained to be a coroner but struggled to keep employment due to erratic behaviour. Not showing up for work, not accepting the authority of his superiors. Once he argued over a cause of death and was so determined to prove himself right that he recovered the body from the morgue and attempted to perform a second post-mortem himself. That was in Philadelphia. He lost that job of course, and shortly afterwards met his Swedish wife and moved here.'

'He was working as a waiter here, wasn't he?"

Nadja nodded. 'He attempted to find work in his field several times in Stockholm, and according to one outburst in an interview believed he was being turned down due to xenophobia and anti-American sentiment. We can only theorise that is why he started killing again.'

'So Ola and Lotta have nothing to do with him?'

Nadja shook her head. 'It does not look that way. There was some skin cells found on the bodies of both Anna Essen and Mattias Eklund, but there was no match in our system so it was of no use to us. Casey Donnantuoro's wife allowed us to take his toothbrush, believing it would prove him innocent. The full tests will take a day or two to complete, but based on initial assessment our lab believes it will be a match. And Henrik —' her voice wavered, she took a shaky breath. 'That post mortem is yet to be completed, of course.'

'There's a summer cottage,' I blurted suddenly. 'Where they go every summer. It's the little boy's favourite place to be. It belongs to his wife's parents, but what if he is hiding out there? It must be empty now. It's pretty remote.'

'Do you know where it is? We can search records but it will take time.'

'The principal of the school has a cottage there too,' I said, pulling my phone out. 'She might know exactly where theirs is.'

40

It wasn't right.

It wasn't right, it wasn't right, it wasn't right.

A policeman was dead. But the killer was locked up. Sigrid could see her. She had been watching her the whole time. Something had gone wrong. She had got confused. It was happening again. It hadn't happened for so many years.

Sigrid paced the floor of her small flat inside the big home that made her feel safe. The social worker would be angry if she saw her like this, picking at her cuticles so roughly that they bled. She would get in trouble. She hated it when people shouted at her. It made her feel as tiny as a mosquito and when she felt tiny, bad things happened. She wound locks of her hair around and around her fingers, so tightly that the tips of her fingers started to bleed.

She closed her eyes and tried to remember the meeting the other night. She had been so powerful, so in control. She had talked and talked and all those people had listened. What had she said? She had said so many words, but they were slipping away now, crumbling into meaningless letters then into dust as she became small like a mosquito.

All the people who came to the meetings would see the real her now, she thought, panic fluttering around her chest like a frightened bird. They would realise that she had been only pretending, that she had barely even understood all the words she had said to them. She didn't know why the woman on the bed was a murderer. She didn't even know if it was true.

Sigrid stopped short so suddenly that she nearly knocked over her favourite photograph, the one of her and the little girl at Christmas one year, after Lisbet had died but before Mamma and Pappa did. They had lied to her. They had told her that the woman on the bed was a dangerous killer who had to be stopped, but it couldn't be true.

They were probably all laughing at her, the stupid old lady who believed what they said. Just like everyone had laughed at her, ever since she was a small child. Sigrid often thought about the fact that she hated people, but she knew the truth deep down. People hated her.

Even the little girl, she realised in dismay. The one person Sigrid had always loved. She must hate her, to have lied to her like this.

41

'Ellie —'

I felt dizzy with exhaustion when I finally stepped out of the police station later that morning. The world swam before my eyes and the only thing I could focus on was Johan. He stood on the front steps, on the opposite side of the building from the area cordoned off by crime scene tape. He looked so familiar and safe that the whole night came crashing over me and suddenly I had collapsed into a heaving, sobbing mess and he gathered me into his arms.

He held me for a long time, almost lifting me off the ground as I buried my face in the soft wool of his winter coat and sobbed and sobbed. Finally I took a shaky breath and stepped back, wiped my face with the hanky he handed me.

'Sorry about that,' I said with a weak smile.

'I heard on the radio news this morning.' He took my red, blotchy face in his hands and kissed my forehead so gently that for a second I thought I might start bubbling all over again. 'They did not name the person who found the detective's body, but I knew it had to be you.'

'He was such a nice guy,' I said, my voice wavering. 'I didn't know him well, I don't have any right to be grieving or anything but it's just so sad. I don't even know if he had a family, or girlfriend or whatever.' I took a shaky breath. 'It's just so sad. I said that already, I'm sorry. I saw the frog, a couple of days ago now. If I'd made the connection earlier —'

'Ellie, no. It was the police's job to catch this killer, and thanks to you, at least they know who he is now.'

I nodded. 'This island where he might be, it isn't big. If he is there, they will catch him any minute.'

'Then that is amazing and you should be proud of yourself.'

I gave a shaky sigh. Nothing felt particularly amazing at the present, but I knew he was right. I was glad he was there.

'Casey asked for me especially to school-in his son. He must have known who I was from last summer. What if it's him that has been in my apartment?'

'Someone has been in your apartment?' Johan stopped short.

'I don't know. Maybe.'

'What? Why didn't you tell me?'

'I wasn't sure. The window was open one night, then another time — I don't know, it was just a feeling. I thought I was just going round the bend, but —' I took a deep breath, trying to gather my thoughts as we started to walk. Johan's arm was firmly around my waist, almost holding me up. 'I'll need to warn my landlady. She's not one for replying to emails, but maybe I could leave a note or something, until they catch him. Maybe she should put off coming home after all.'

'We are going to your apartment now to collect your stuff

and you are coming home today. You cannot stay there any more."

'Johan you don't need to do that.'

'It is only two days until you were coming back anyway, right?'

There was a note of uncertainty in his voice that made me stop.

'I thought —' I began.

I looked away. A daycare class of ten or fifteen pre schoolers, some in pairs, others holding hands with teachers, toddled by, matching luminous pink vests covering their rain gear. A little girl with long plaits sticking out from beneath her woolly hat broke formation to leap into a puddle of slush, and I half-smiled as I heard the exhausted teacher try to patiently explain why she must stay with the group when there were cars nearby.

'*Men jag vill!*' the toddler argued in a high pitched but determined voice. But I want to.

At the back of the group a teacher held hands with a wobbly toddler with scraggly ginger curls that reminded me of Tor-Björn.

As one of the teachers started to sing a rousing marching song, I tore my eyes away from them and back to Johan. Maybe I should leave this conversation until I had had some sleep. Everything felt a bit hazy and surreal, though I was surprisingly calm. I had to do it now. *In for a penny in for a pound*, I thought, taking a deep breath.

'I thought maybe you didn't want me to,' I said in a rush. 'That maybe you — maybe it's all been too much, for us. Maybe it was too late to start again.'

'Do you still love me?'

I nodded, not quite able to speak.

'I love you,' he said simply, and the lump in my throat

grew. 'For these last few months, I didn't really know what I thought or felt. Losing Liv, and thinking about my father for the first time in so many years. And losing Mia,' he added quietly. 'I have felt like I was in a — what's the word again, a clothes dryer, you know? Going round and round and sometimes upside down, being tossed against these horrible truths over and over and not really being able to see anything beyond them. But the only thing I could see clearly the whole time was you. I have not done enough lately to deserve you, but I am going to change that.'

I managed a wobbly smile. 'I'm willing to give you that chance.'

'Thank you.'

'You're welcome.'

'This is me,' I said as we turned into my road. It wasn't particularly likely that Casey Donnantuoro would be slinking around in broad daylight, but still I scanned the road as I took my glove off to key in the front door code. The street was empty.

'Ellie — I don't understand. This is where you have been living?'

'Yes, so?'

'What apartment?'

I never understood the expression 'white as a sheet' until that moment. The colour drained from Johan's face as he stared at me in horror.

'Third floor, far left as you come out of the elevator.'

'That is Mia's apartment.'

42

Gabriella Martinez was fairly confident that there were few things more boring in life than being assigned to guard a guy in a coma. Most of her team were racing out to the archipelago island where a sighting of Casey Donnantuoro had now been reported, and here she was hanging around a hospital corridor watching over a piece-of-shit wife killer who would probably never wake up. She was positive she had been stuck with the dud job because she had questioned her boss and made him look an idiot in the team meeting this morning. The fact that it wasn't difficult to make him look an idiot really wasn't her problem.

Gabriella yawned and glanced at her watch. Three more hours and she would be off duty. She had told Brita and Lia she would join them for cocktails at one of the Stureplan bars they liked to hang out at to flirt with older men, but already she knew she would make macaroni and cheese and eat it in front of the TV. This job was making her old before her time, she thought with a sigh.

She loved the flash of respect she saw in men's eyes

when she told them what she did for a living. Then there would be the inevitable quip about how she could handcuff them if she wanted, but if they were really cute she would forgive it. The truth she hadn't admitted to anyone yet, even herself, however, was that the police force had turned out to be a lot more work and less fun than she had envisioned, and she was probably no more than two or three more shifts like this away from quitting.

That would annoy her parents, who would remind her she couldn't live at home rent-free even if she wasn't working, and warn her she had better not get up to her old tricks again of going dancing and staying out all hours with men they didn't even know. Gabriella rolled her eyes at the very thought of the conversation, then, keeping half an eye on the door behind which Ola Andersson lay dead to the world, she snuck half way up the corridor to the vending machine.

She really wasn't supposed to leave her post without informing hospital security who would come and relieve her officially, but for heaven's sake it was only a few metres, and the guy was unconscious. What exactly was going to happen in the thirty seconds it would take her to buy yet another bag of chips? This was the other problem with boring shifts, Gabriella thought ruefully as she wandered back. A few more shifts like this and she'd be sweating salt and vinegar.

'There you are, quick — he is speaking and I think a police officer needs to hear this.' The nurse turned and ran towards the room, and Gabriella dropped her chips in her haste to grab the little notebook she was supposed to use to log anything official.

A weary looking Indian doctor was shining a light in Ola

Andersson's eyes as he wriggled like Gabriella's cat when she tried to give him medicine.

'Get away, get away from me —' he was muttering in a hoarse voice. They must have already taken the intubation tube out. Shit — how long had she dawdled at the vending machine? She'd only sent three texts.

'What was he saying?' she snapped with what she hoped sounded like authority.

'Something about a woman?'

'Ola — can you hear me? I am officer Gabriella Martinez. What do you want to say about a woman?'

'She told me — told me it was her.'

'Who told you? Lotta Berglund?'

'No!' he shouted. 'She is the killer. She said so.'

'Somebody else told you that Lotta Berglund was the killer?'

'Makes sense. Why else would she be such a bitch?'

'Who? Who told you?'

He smirked suddenly. 'My first.' His face twitched as though he was trying to laugh but his face had forgotten how. 'Perks of being a ski instructor.'

43

Johan snipped through the mesh wire and yanked open a hole big enough for he and I to climb into Mia's attic. Swedish apartment building attics are divided up amongst residents in sort of mesh wire cages, so everyone has a few cubic metres each to store their junk. The police had searched Mia's months earlier, but we had to do something. There might just be something that only someone who knew Mia as well as Johan did would understand the significance of.

That, and I suspected Johan was keeping me busy to keep my mind off things. Nadja had promised to text me when they arrested Casey Donnantuoro. Though my phone was on its loudest setting, I couldn't help but double check it every three seconds. So far, nothing.

And even that was better than thinking about why Mia had wanted me in her apartment. To keep an eye on me? Had she been listening in on me? I kept thinking over every conversation I'd had in the flat, every blether with my mum about rubbish, every sweet nothing with Johan, catch ups with Kate, Henrik, Marty MacDonald in Boston. It must have been her that opened my window that night, her who had been standing in the doorway the night I'd thought I had a nightmare.

Icy terror slithered around me, squeezed me tight at the thought, but she hadn't hurt me. She had had access to me, fast asleep, more or less every night for more than three months. So what the hell did she want with me?

The attic was impeccably neat, with everything divided into storage boxes of the appropriate size and labelled. Johan was flicking through a box of school yearbooks.

'That is Karin Söderström,' he told me, pointing to a picture of a shy looking teenager standing at the edge of a group. 'The school librarian. Mia was one too.'

'Mia was a school librarian?' I tried to smile but I knew my voice was shrill. 'She's not predictable, I'll give her that.'

'What name did she give you as the landlady?'

I opened my phone to dig out the original email correspondence.

'Here it is,' I said finally. 'Sigrid Johansson. I remember thinking it was a sign because there was a Johan in it.'

He smiled briefly. 'That is her aunt, I think. There is something not quite right about her mind. I don't know the details, but she lives in some sort of residence which Mia pays for. Mia's mother died when she was a baby.'

He rummaged in a box of photograph albums and pulled one out. 'Somewhere in here there should be — '

He handed me the album, pointed to a photograph of a teenaged Mia with a lady with long white hair. I frowned. I'd seen her before. *Don't you want to be safe?* The woman addressing the group. The vigilantes.

'That's it —' I said, my heart racing as it started to fall in to place. 'The profiler was right. This is Mia's next kill. High profile, showing off her power. The victim is Lotta Bergland.'

44

Dumb and stupid. Everybody was dumb and stupid, and so, finally was Casey Donnantuoro. For the first time in his life he had made a mistake and now he was going to pay.

The wind shrieked in and out of the old building as a wild storm blew in from the Baltic Sea. Casey Donnantuoro crouched in the cellar beneath his wife's family's *sommarstuga* and waited for the moment he was going to be blown to kingdom come. He could see maggots, roaches, scuttling back and forth across the ceiling, then he remembered that it was too dark to see anything. The maggots and roaches were in his mind. Maybe they would eat him before the police got him.

'Casey, please come out.'

A *woman*? They got a freaking chick cop to try to negotiate with *him*?

'You are not in any danger. Please keep calm, and walk slowly up the stairs. You will not be hurt.'

Casey laughed and laughed. Not in any danger? He had killed four goddamned people including a freaking cop. He pumped their bodies full of embalming fluid and he posed them in the city to give people nightmares. The second he showed his head above those stairs, they were going to blow it right off.

Which is how it was always going to be. He knew that. He accepted it. He wasn't afraid of dying. He never had been. He'd thought about doing it himself, a bunch of times. He used to play with his dad's guns in the basement in Lawrence, Massachusetts, sometimes letting a loaded one drop just to see what would happen. He'd climb out his bedroom window onto the sloped roof of his family's three storey colonial and just sit there, dangling ever closer to the edge until some neighbourhood girls started to shriek and then he'd laugh. He even once drank the contents of a test tube in a high school chemistry class, and couldn't stop cracking up at the teacher's terror, even while his throat burned and he felt like his eyes would pop out.

But none of those times, did he die, so he figured he was supposed to be alive. Then he started to figure there must be a purpose. He had to know something he was supposed to share with the world. Except nobody would ever listen to him because he was a loser.

Until the night he followed Jason Winslow. He never knew why he followed people. He just did it sometimes. Girls, guys. Old people, kids. Who cared. They were all the same. But he followed Jason Winslow as he walked his date home, and when Jason Winslow kissed her good night, Casey started to feel a little weird.

She was pretty. The kind of girl Casey never even really got to see up close. The kind of girl that moved away as soon as she saw Casey coming. He'd seen them on TV though, he knew what they were like. Shiny hair you could grab a fistful off, tight asses. Lips Casey always figured had to taste like strawberries or cherries or something from that glossy stuff they put on them. Lips that Jason Winslow got to taste, while Casey just imagined.

It wasn't like it was the first time Casey discovered that guys like Jason Winslow got access to a kind of life that Casey would always be denied, but for some reason that was the night he was done putting up with it. It was also the night he had a little vial in his pocket that he'd taken from the morgue.

When he slipped it into his pocket, he'd vaguely thought he might drink it himself. It had been a while since he tested his own mortality. But when Jason Winslow left the girl and started to walk down the street, all cocky like he owned the world — and no wonder, Casey had seen exactly what he had just gotten to squeeze under the girl's sweater — Casey decided it was time he tested someone else's mortality.

And man, it was fuckin' messy. Jason Winslow was a big guy, and he didn't die easy. Casey had thought a little about looking for work as an executioner in prisons, but if they were all this hard work then he was out. He was incapacitated quickly enough, but that fuckin' heart would not stop beating for most of the night. Casey had injected him with a lot more than he ever meant to before he finally felt his pulse weaken and die and he was so exhausted he could hardly even enjoy the triumph. That was when he realised he wasn't done having fun with Jason Winslow.

He'd gotten a lot better at it since then.

Over a lot of cities. He didn't always pose them out in the snow, but he liked to when he could. He'd never been good at building snowmen as a kid, they always seemed to crumble and kind of collapse before he was even done making them, but his ice statues never crumbled or collapsed. He liked them. They made him happy. All the news headlines and groups of crazies freaking out all over the city all because of him, It had been a trip. It had been worth it.

Even if it was over now.

Before he could lose his nerve, Casey scrabbled from his hiding place and raced up the stairs, bracing himself for the shower of bullets.

'Okay I'm glad you decided to come up. Can you get on your knees, please?'

What? Where was his shower of bullets? Did this bit just say *please?* To him?

'Just stay calm, everything will be okay. Are you hurt?'

'No I'm not freaking hurt!' Casey yelled, and his voice went that high pitched way it always did when he was upset. Kids laughed at him, his mom beat him for sounding like a girl. And these assholes just stood calmly watching him in silence.

'Shoot me!' he screamed. 'Shoot me!'

'There is no reason for us to shoot you. We are seven people and you are one. You pose no threat to us. Please get on your knees and put your hands in the air.'

Somehow Casey found himself obeying. After a moment, he felt the cool metal of handcuffs and then he was pulled, gently but firmly to his feet and walked to a waiting cop car. It was the biggest anti-climax of his life.

45

'The group — Anki said they were going to take action after another murder. Henrik is the next murder. They are going to kill Lotta.'

I hissed urgently over my shoulder as I clattered down the stairs from the attic back to my flat — Mia's flat, with Johan right behind me. My bloody phone battery was at 2% so I grabbed my charger to plug it in before scrolling to Nadja's number.

'This whole thing has been some kind of — I don't even know, play, to prove that she is cleverer than all of us.'

'I should have known,' Johan said quietly, with a bitter smile. 'Mia never liked to lose.'

'Those pamphlets in your kitchen — Johan —'

Nadja wasn't answering. She must be still pursuing Casey Donnantuoro. What should I do now? Was this something I could call the usual emergency number with?

'Krister,' he said. 'Krister has joined the group. I was not happy about it, but I thought maybe, hopefully it would help him a little. Give him a place to channel his anger. Ellie

— he is with them tonight. Something is happening tonight.'

'Did he join because of Mia?'

Johan shook his head. 'I am certain he doesn't know. He talked about it all to me the night you went out to get pizza. He is not a good liar. He went to their meetings to try to get over Mia. Shit. *Vad fan, Krister,*' he muttered under his breath.

'Call him,' I said. 'Warn him. As soon asI get through to Nadja — though what's the point? We have no idea where they are, where Lotta is.'

'Wait —' Johan said. 'We have an app that shows us where the other's phone is. It's from a trip we took years ago, but I don't think we ever disconnected — yes.' Johan frowned. 'He is in one of the old disused factories at Hammarby. They are all condemned.'

'That must be where they're holding her. Let's go. I'll keep calling Nadja.'

We both ran for the door —

'Johan, how are we going to get there? It's rush hour, the traffic will be bumper to bumper.'

'I have an idea,' he said.

46

Lotta Berglund stirred from a deep sleep and for a moment she thought she was drowning. Her voice was hoarse as she fought for breath, every cell in her body felt limp and weak, her lungs too exhausted to expand no matter how hard she tried. The fever had come, finally, and it had not been the relief she had hoped for.

The darkness was still complete, but Lotta was used to that now. She had almost forgotten what light was like. The thought of being able to see anything beyond the end of her nose terrified her.

So this is what it is like to die, she thought. She didn't feel too badly. The exhaustion, the sensation of being drained of every last scrap of energy, was strangely pleasant. Relaxing. All the terror was gone, her adrenaline spent.

There was no torturing herself with decisions of whether to fight or run when they came for her. The prospect of doing either was laughable. She would simply lie here and wait until it was over.

People talked of what they would regret on their deathbeds. The general consensus was that no one would ever wish they had done more work, but Lotta did. She wished she had had that breakthrough. She wished she had gritted her teeth and kept with the Boston project.

She wished she had never ranted about it the first night she got back to Sweden in that bar. It wasn't the sort of place Lotta would ever have gone into normally. She had lived in Stockholm her entire life without setting foot on Stureplan. But when the plane landed, Lotta was still as angry as she had been when it took off, so she took the Arlanda Express to Stockholm's Central Station and then walked and walked until the glow of a candle on a table inside a restaurant caught her eye and she walked in to sit near it.

They didn't want her there. She wasn't dressed like the women there, with their tight jeans and high heels and artfully tousled curls. Also, none of them carried a gigantic, battered, suitcase. The hostess, or whatever you called it, came over, all fake smiles, and asked Lotta if she would like a menu. No, she would not like a menu, thank you, but also she declined to leave, just yet.

So then another woman came over. A manager? Who knows. Tall and blonde and perfect like all the others, but this one listened to Lotta. Lotta poured out the whole story and the woman seemed sympathetic, fascinated. She asked so many questions, and Lotta was too tired and heartsick to care.

Until a few weeks ago. Lotta had been travelling so much over the past six months or so, attending a conference in Denver, guest lecturing at the University of Cape Town, even fitting in a few days' hiking in Iceland, that she hadn't paid a great deal of attention to the news in Sweden. But on the plane back from South Africa, she flicked through the online version of a Swedish newspaper and came across a long article about the Södermalm Murders that were revealed last summer.

Lotta instantly knew what drug had been used. She just had to find the woman she had spoken to that night. And then she had woken up here.

Lotta finally realised what had woken her. Voices. Footsteps. Clanking.

They were coming for her, but when they opened the door, she was pleased to note that she didn't feel an ounce of gratitude. She had been right about Stockholm Syndrome.

47

They have her. I don't even have to wait for someone to tell me, I can hear it from here. The excited chatter, the surge of anticipation.

It is a palpable thing. We like to talk of emotions as though they don't truly exist, as though they are imaginary and can be changed at will. But emotions are electrical impulses just like any other. Each fires into the atmosphere and makes its little mark regardless of whether the feeling was direct or confused, healthy or destructive. Or created entirely by me.

If Lotta has worked it out, she will think it's because she threatened to expose me. She posed on several noticeboards she must have deduced I frequented, cryptic references to our meeting and suggesting that if I did not give her an explanation she would go to the police. But she posed no threat to me. Ellie already told them it was me, and yet here I am.

The circumstances of my life have changed, but the facade of normality was never going to last forever. For months, even before Ellie arrived, I felt my true self trying to burst out. Liv was worried about me. She thought I was unhappy with Krister as she had been with Johan. When she held my hand and promised *she would support me whatever I chose to do, it took everything in me not to laugh in her face. I laughed in the end, though. Her face as she understood what was happening milliseconds before she died is a delicious memory I have held to myself ever since.*

Almost as delicious as these months of listening to Ellie. Hearing her lie and lie and lie. Everything's fab! Loving life. All great with Johan. Big adventure. I'm on the trail of a serial killer.

Except you never were, Ellie. You were just picking up the breadcrumbs I left out for you like a good little puppet. Gifting Tove's mother a computer so she could find pictures I had planted on her old one was a particular stroke of genius.

Admittedly you found the American, but he was hardly a challenge. He was a child, doing cartwheels in the grass. Mamma, pappa! Look at me! Look what I can do!

If only he could have controlled himself a little better so that my aunt didn't have to die. Giving her the phone was a mistake. I thought it would keep her busy, keep her focussed, when I could see her starting to slip. She's always started to slip, sooner or later, ever since I was a little girl. That is the difference between her and me. I never slip.

Good bye, Sigrid, I think now, as I step over her body. It has been a long time since I felt my special syringe slide into the neck of someone I had chosen. Too long. I had forgotten just how nice it felt. Was Liv really the last one? Goodness.

Not long until another one now. It's not a thrill that slips through me, simply acceptance. This is who I am and this is what must happen. I can no more control it than I can a tsunami or earthquake. We all must die. It is nothing personal.

But if Lotta thinks that this is my revenge, she is very wrong. I did not do this for fear of who she could tell about me. I did all this just for fun.

48

Johan was a helluva lot better at cycling through melting ice than me. He zipped around corners in a controlled skid, wove around frozen puddles without breaking speed, while I slithered and slid and generally came within a hair's breadth of breaking my neck every block or so.

We'd flown around Ringvägen and were climbing Skanstull bridge. The lights of Hammarby were twinkling ahead, our way was lit like tiny, resentful beacons of brake lights glowing red, two by two through the drizzle as far as the eye could see. I'd got through to the emergency number and was trying and failing to make the situation understood when Nadja must have seen all the missed calls from me and called back. They had Casey Donnantuoro under arrest and were making their way back to the city.

Nadja was sending a local team directly to the old factory and would catch up herself as soon as she could. I'd declined to mention that Johan and I were on our way too. She could find out that bit of information in good time.

'This way!' Johan's voice was almost eaten by the wind,

but I saw him swerve off to the right and onto a dirt pathway that wound along the waterfront towards the factory where Krister was.

'Shit —' My bike skidded out from under me and I was deposited in an ungainly heap in a prickly push.

'Are you okay?'

'I'm fine — keep going — I'll catch up!' I yelled. He hesitated, then did as he was told. I yanked the bike to a standing position, and gritting my teeth got back on. 'Come on fucker, don't let me down,' I muttered under my. breath. This little bit of pathway was treacherously steep and the worst place to remount, but I didn't have the time to hesitate, I hoped on and hoped for the best and somehow I was back in business.

I could only just spy the reflectors of Johan's bike in the distance as I pedalled as fast as I could after him. I hit rocks and ice and stones but somehow absorbed each skid to pedal on. My jeans were soaked through and there was a dark stain spreading on my knee where I must have burst the skin when I fell. Everything was burning, everything was throbbing, I felt as though I'd gone into another dimension of physical misery when I finally spied Johan's bike hang a sharp left.

The huge factory loomed high overhead, black against the purple sky, and even if I couldn't see the lights of people moving around the yard, the throb of horrified, excited chatter, I would have known it was the right place. I could almost taste the malignant energy. This is her lair, I thought. This is where she has been hiding out all this time.

At a half crumbled wall, Johan had stopped. He leaned his bike against it, careful not to make any noise, though I suspected no one would have heard. I stuck mine against his, and he took my hand as we both crept towards a gap in the wall.

Though I had had a rough idea of what to expect, nothing could have prepared me for the sight that greeted us. An old cobblestoned yard, bordered by once imposing, now mostly crumbled, walls, was flooded with silver light, casting an eerie glow over the gathering. There was a small platform in the centre of the yard, it looked as though it had once been a fishpond or fountain, now boarded over.

A crowd of people, normal, standard people I'd stood next to in lines for coffee, waiting for the T-bana, held doors for, were crowded round the platform like a mediaeval mob, baying for blood. I couldn't understand the low Swedish chant, but fuck I could comprehend it, and the sheer, palpable malevolence stabbed at my spine like electric shocks. One or two of them were even holding mobile phones where their pitchforks should be, filming the horror.

Hatred etched on their faces turned them into human gargoyles. They began to sway, as one, seemed almost about to break into some Bacchus-like frenzy of vitriol when suddenly they parted. Someone was moving through them.

'Mia,' breathed Johan. I squeezed his hand as Mia walked through the crowd to the little platform. She was followed by two people supporting a third, staggering, barely conscious woman I took to be Lotta Berglund. On her left was the guy with the long hair who had approached me. On her right — it was Corinna.

Mia reached the platform and held up her hands for silence. She said something, though her back to us and we couldn't catch the words. But we did catch the next word.

'Mia.'

Krister stepped forward, ashen, staring at his former girlfriend in horror.

'He is saying she cannot do this,' Johan whispered. I nodded. I'd caught it more or less. 'That it's not too late. If she turns herself in he will support her —'

Mia threw back her head and laughed and some of the crowd joined in.

'Please, Mia, listen —' Johan muttered, Krister ignored the jeers, his face set in a determined, blank stare. 'It doesn't have to be like this. You don't have to be like this. Come with me now and I will protect you.'

'Do you think he means it?' I whispered.

'I don't know,' said Johan.

Just then sirens were heard, approaching fast, and the crowd scattered with a flurry of screams and frantic shoves. As the sirens got louder, Corinna and the guy scarpered too, leaving poor Lotta slumped on the platform. Neither Mia nor Krister moved.

Johan began to creep forward.

The police cars were still a few blocks away, I judged. I could see the syringe glinting in the light in Mia's hand. The drug was instantaneous. If she got to Johan —

But she showed no sign of being aware of him.

She was staring at Krister, transfixed.

'You would help me?' she asked in Swedish. 'Even now?'

'Always,' Krister said. 'I promised, didn't I? Forever.'

'Even though you know what I am?'

'Forever,' he repeated, firmly.

Her hand holding the syringe relaxed and Johan lunged forward, grabbed her in a headlock as she struggled viciously. I ran to Lotta, checked her pulse. She stirred weakly, groaned. The sirens were deafening.

'Over here!' I screamed. I spied the first couple of

uniformed officers approaching but they still seemed a million miles away. I heard Johan grunt as Mia bit him, then Krister was there. He grabbed her ankles and the two of them wrestled her to the ground.

'We need an ambulance —' I yelled.

'There is one just behind us, please stay calm —' It was the same no nonsense young woman who'd been first to respond when I found Mattias Eklund. Her partner seemed no more up to the task than he had then.

I heard Johan yell and realised he must have loosened his grip on Mia for an instant — with super human strength she wriggled from his grasp and to her feet.

The officer with the plait pulled out her gun, yelled at her to freeze but Mia sprinted to the edge of the yard and clambered onto the high fence at the edge of the water.

'No — Mia —' Krister ran for her. 'Please Mia, no —'

A bullet ricocheted off one of the iron bars of the fence as Mia yanked herself over and flung herself into the black waters of Årstaviken.

There was an instant of stillness, of silence as we all stared at the spot from which she had disappeared. Then the two police officers sprang into action, the paramedics arrived and took charge of Lotta. My breath heaved in my chest as I struggled to my feet and staggered over to Johan, wondering why he hadn't moved yet.

It was then that I noticed the syringe sticking out of his jeans leg.

Hi!

Thank you so much for reading *Broken Mirrors!* I really hope you enjoyed it and don't hate me too much for the cliffhanger :-)

Panic not, because I am hard at work on the Stockholm Murders Book 3 and you'll have it before the end of 2019.

In the meantime, you can pop over to my Facebook group: https://www.facebook.com/groups/csduffywriter/ where I share news of upcoming releases and we're often chatting about crime fiction - either mine or someone else's!

Also feel free to drop me a line: claire@csduffy-writer.com I respond to all emails, though sometimes it takes me a while!

Thanks again for reading - and if you get a moment to pop a review on Amazon or Goodreads I won't be mad!!

Claire xx

ABOUT THE AUTHOR

C.S. Duffy writes crime thrillers with a healthy dose of black humour. Her background is in film and TV, and she has several projects in development in Sweden and the UK, including the feature film *Guilty*. She is the author of *Life is Swede,* a thriller in the form of a blog - leading several readers to contact Swedish news agencies asking them why they hadn't reported the murder that features in the blog. Her supernatural audio series is currently running on Storytel in several countries and she was selected as Spotlight author at Bloody Scotland in 2018.

www.csduffywriter.com

Printed in Great Britain
by Amazon